A STRANGE CASE FOR INSPECTOR DYLAN WALKER

PHOBIAS

MANUEL J. SPENCER

PHOBIAS

A STRANGE CASE FOR INSPECTOR DYLAN WALKER

Copyright ©2024 – Manuel J. Spencer

ALL RIGHTS RESERVED

Sommario

Dylan Walker 5

The strange case of Lisa Lawson 10

Sally Smith 13

Nothing good 20

Eureka! 23

A special mission 27

Seeking confirmation 31

From dusk to dawn 36

There is no needle in the haystack 43

Professor Benjamin Hunt 47

Well done David! 53

Positive feelings 57

Something does not add up 61

Claustrophobia 70

The Roman London Museum 76

Old Man Hunt 86

Autophobia 91

Alan Baker 97

Tomophobia 101

A half-truth 107

No breaks, Inspector Walker! 111

Nothing new 118

Vicky Williams 124

Acrophobia 128

Mr. Mystery 134

O.C.D. 140

Dylan Walker

Friday, 22 February 2019.

This one just didn't take.

It was just after five in the afternoon and less than half an hour to the end of his shift. Inspector Dylan Walker was already looking forward to returning home, where, like every Friday evening, his three children, Janet, John and Jack, would be waiting for him, their hands no doubt already floured and ready to knead the pizza.

It was at that very moment that the phone rang.

On the other end of the receiver, Sergeant David Carter, in an unusually alarmed tone, informed him that he would have to reach him urgently at James Barry's Hospital. It was not easy for him to understand anything else, both because of the confusing noises in the background and because the line suddenly went dead.

It was wicked weather outside, with wind and rain sweeping through the streets since the early hours of the morning, which had created quite a few communication problems throughout the day. He couldn't remember how long it had been since he had last seen such a dreary sky. But he had known Sergeant Carter all his life and knew well when there was no time to waste. Despite everything, his thoughts returned for a moment to the warmth of his home where the three little brats were waiting for him in vain.

"Not again and then there's pizza tonight!" - he thought to himself as, after getting up from his desk, he grabbed his mackintosh with one hand and with the other tried to send a text message to his wife to warn her that he would be late.

The pizza would have to wait.

For a Londoner this might have seemed a rather strange habit, but everyone who knew Dylan was well aware of his passion for Italian cuisine. It was no coincidence that ten years earlier he had been married to Sara, a girl from Italy whom he had met at Subway, a pub in Hackbridge, a suburb of the London Borough of Sutton, where he had had to intervene following an anonymous phone call reporting nocturnal disturbances. Sara was undocumented as she had inadvertently left them at the hotel and it was far from easy for Dylan to convince the young woman to follow him to the station for identification. At around six feet tall, the girl made no small spectacle of holding her own against an officer like Dylan who towered over her by at least twenty-five centimetres. It was a scene bordering on the comical with that petite Italian who, not knowing a single word of English, tried to communicate with large, quick hand movements.

Dylan had always enjoyed the funny stories about Italians gesticulating while talking but he was not at all prepared for such a situation and especially that little hurricane. That night Sara never made it to the station for identification and the situation was so clear that, in the days that followed, none of those who were present at Subway were surprised to see them walking together again through the streets of the village. Sara prolonged her stay on English soil by lodging in a hostel but soon moved into Dylan's house who, when her parents asked for an explanation, passed her off as an Italian second cousin of a close friend of his who was looking for accommodation for his studies. Dylan had never been good at lying but that excuse worked particularly well for him and he was still very proud of it. It was only three years before the two decided to pledge their love for the rest of their lives.

They were indeed a beautiful couple, Dylan Walker and Sara Di Giulio, thirty-two years old he and twenty-seven years old she, two young people who were warmly welcomed into the Hackbridge community. For obvious reasons related to Dylan's job, they decided to buy a house in that very area, not far from where they had met, on Longfield Avenue.

Hackbridge was a very quiet suburb, considered by many to be ideal for starting a family and raising children peacefully. Sara soon managed to adapt to the English way of life, incorporating into the family's customs and traditions that hint of Italianism that made her special in everyone's eyes.

The house was modest in size, on two floors, with an attic that they used as a storage room and a small outdoor area of their own, enclosed with a gate. A very pretty arrangement that, with the passage of time, had become far too crowded: in fact the little princess Janet was followed three years later by the twins John and Jack, the little men of the house who were now already five years old. It was because of them that poor Jack Sparrow, a three-year-old Manchester Terrier, had to give up any pretense of living in the house constantly. Dylan was adamant this time, but Sara's disapproving look and Janet's screams forced him to set up a kennel resembling a small palace in the outdoor area, complete with artificial grass and play area, which cost him half a salary and a bad back for the next ten days.

Dylan had also done very well with impeccable conduct within the Met, the Metropolitan Police Service. Only four years earlier he had been appointed an inspector and transferred to the newly formed S.I.P. division of the Southern Police District of London. The Special Investigation Police was a special unit in support of the Met, set up mainly to deal with the most complex cases, consisting of two independent teams, located respectively in the south and north of the City, and reporting to headquarters in Westminster. The headquarters of the South London detachment, headed by Chief Inspector Martin Cooper, was in Hackbridge, on Fellnex Avenue and had about four hundred officers. The task of Dylan and his S.I.P. colleagues had, until then, been limited to surveillance and support of the other police forces, since, in those four years, no cases of particular interest arose.

To be honest, uptown, people were already beginning to think that it was a superfluous unit and rumours had begun to circulate that, by the end of the year, many officers would be transferred to counter-terrorism. When word spread that Inspector Walker had bought a house on Longfield Avenue, all the residents on the street were nevertheless delighted to have a law enforcement representative as a neighbour.

And they were even more so when, on the first Friday in August, Sara used to invite the whole neighbourhood to eat her pizza. A simple act of courtesy had immediately turned into a challenge to the death between Sara's pizza and the barbecue of Mrs Grace, who lived a little further down the street, in a nice little house with a large private garden. This year would be the tenth edition and the winner had not yet been decided. To be honest, all the jurors would have done anything not to deliver a verdict that could have marked the end of two of the most anticipated summer events of the year. Of course for Dylan there was no contest, he was crazy about Sara's pizza and wouldn't miss it for the world.

Not for anything in the world, except for the fateful call of Sergeant Carter whom he considered, at the same time, both his greatest friend and the greatest calamity he had ever encountered in his life.

David Carter, forty-one years old and single by no choice of his own, was a big man weighing over a hundred kilos by six feet, a trouble magnet to say the least, and not a day went by without him messing something up. He was at his best then when he was off duty and still acted like he did when they were boys and would hang around the pubs hoping for a sweet conquest. Only David was as comfortable with the fairer sex as an orangutan would be in a glassware shop. Punctually he would find himself partying late into the night and, the next morning, Dylan would have to work up a sweat to be able to justify his tardiness, his upside-down jumper or his rather scruffy appearance. Sergeant Carter was known by his colleagues as the special missions man, because the excuse most often used by Dylan to justify his delays was that he had sent him somewhere on the planet to find some clue about who knows what. David had with his quirks, unintentionally, the ability to start a long working day with a smile and for that he was well liked by all. He was a good man and would bend over backwards for anyone, and for Dylan he would even give his own life. Uncle David was also the most beloved belly of the Walker household and considered Dylan's family to be his family, Jack Sparrow to be his dog and even Dylan's sofa to be his. In fact, Dylan's couch was really his couch, as David often took possession of it at the end of dinner and, starting to hum, spent the whole night there, ready to enjoy, the next morning, the famous maple syrup pancakes Sara used to make for the kids.

"This morning double ration..." - These few whispered words from Sara were enough to make Dylan realise that David, bulkier than ten Jack Sparrows, was once again left sleeping on their sofa in the living room.

The strange case of Lisa Lawson

As he drove towards James Barry's Hospital, with the windscreen wipers sweeping at top speed the drops of water violently beating on the windscreen, he was reminded of the strange case of Lisa Lawson. He promised himself that he would also ask about her once he arrived at the hospital to find out from the direct voice of Dr. Anthony Green if there were any signs of improvement. He really hoped that the doctor was on duty since he had not heard from poor Lisa for at least two days. For a moment he had even hoped that the news was about that unfortunate girl, but David's tone of voice had alerted his sixth sense and he was already clear on two things: this was going to be a new case and it certainly wasn't any good.

Dylan had already spent the whole of the previous Saturday night at James Barry's Hospital in a desperate attempt to gather some valuable information but arrived at dawn with the realisation that he had not been able to get a spider's web out of the hole. In the early afternoon of that Saturday a young girl had been found unconscious, just under the small bridge where the Hackbridge Road crosses the River Wandle. It had been a beautiful day at the end of February, and an excessively warm sun for the time had raised the temperature just enough to draw cyclists, runners and all lovers of riverside walks to the road. It was an unhoped-for respite in that cold winter and the day seemed to be off to a good start.

Dylan, too, had planned a short family outing to visit Uncle Jimmy in Kings Hill where, perhaps taking advantage of the fine weather, he would be able to shoot a round at Kings Hill Golf Club. The ubiquitous David would join them as usual, as he wouldn't miss for the world both Aunt Amber's Red Velvet cake and the chance to finally give that cocky Dylan a golf lesson.

When his name appeared on the smartphone display in the early afternoon, Dylan had thought she was contacting him just to throw down the usual gauntlet. He smiled, as it would be the usual pointless provocation because David, the king of 'air shots', had never beaten him at golf and never could! Obviously, those two days went contrary to what he had planned and David not only did not challenge him but did not even give him good news.

The alarm had been raised by a cyclist who, having just entered the cycle path on the side of the bridge leading to The Wrythe, had accidentally noticed a body lying prone in the vegetation and had promptly alerted the emergency medical services. Undergoing initial treatment in an ambulance, the girl was already awake when she arrived at the hospital, but was in a state of severe shock and unresponsive to any external stimuli.

Once the doctors had given their approval, Dylan joined her in her room and gently tried to get any information, to find out who she was, as no one had yet reported her missing and, above all, how she had ended up under that bridge and in that state. The night, under the watchful eye of Dr Green, passed without the poor girl uttering a single word. All Dylan knew at the time was that the girl had been in a catatonic state caused by post-traumatic shock for the next three days, according to the doctors.

It was discovered in the early hours of the next morning, thanks to the missing persons report filed by her parents, that her name was Lisa Lawson and she lived not far from where she was found. She was a 21-year-old model student, very reserved and who liked to spend her days alternating her studies with a good dose of physical activity, either by walking along the banks of the River Wandle or doing free body exercises at Dale Park. A very beautiful girl indeed, but exaggeratedly introverted and, according to her parents, with very few friends and whom she very seldom dated anyway. Her attitudes were such as to denote a girl who at the age of 21 had not yet severed the umbilical cord.

The investigations were still at a standstill, also because the doctors had found no signs on the patient that were compatible with beatings or trauma and, in addition, the girl continued to spend her days sitting on the edge of the bed, always facing the window and with her gaze fixed, lost in emptiness.

No one from the station had even tried to hint at a possible hypothesis and it was a common belief that only Lisa Lawson would be able to unravel the mystery surrounding her, if she ever came to her senses one day.

In the early days, the press had enjoyed splashing such a peculiar news story across the front page, peppered with a variety of theories put forward by self-styled experts who were nothing more than the usual charlatans looking for a minute of fleeting glory. When he had been assigned the case, Dylan never thought he would find himself in such an entangled situation.

"Well, the crazies will all be yours!" - Chief Inspector Cooper told him after his arrival at S.I.P. as soon as he heard he had a degree in psychology.

Dylan loved to study and read in his spare time but now he was aware that this time studying would not help him solve the case. Without the slightest clue, he was convincing himself that perhaps no one would ever find out the truth and the Lisa Lawson case would sooner or later join the list of unsolved cases.

Sally Smith

James Barry's Hospital was an impressive, newly built hospital located on the London Road in the Beddington Park area. It soon managed to distinguish itself in London's health care scene because it offered its users a high standard of care and high-quality services. The facility was one of the jewels in the crown for the small Hackbridge community and was also home to the New London Children's Hospital, a paediatric hospital specialising in the treatment of childhood and childhood illnesses. Nothing was left to chance and even the site chosen for its construction was identified with the help of top medical professionals. The main structure, only three storeys high, overlooked the London Road but then extended inland into Beddington Park. It was a futuristic hospital, surrounded by greenery, optimised to shorten the duration of the diagnostic and therapeutic course, to minimise the length of stay and thus have a positive impact on the patient's quality of life.

From James Barry's Hospital it was possible to access the park through three small gates on three sides of the outdoor garden and it was not uncommon to see relatives and friends of hospital patients taking advantage of this for a moment of relaxation. Beddington Park was also a favourite destination for local residents to take long, refreshing walks. There were various paths within the park, but the most popular were the paths that ran along the banks of the River Wandle and crossed the park from east to west. Of the various parks in the greater London area, Beddington Park was considered to be one of the major archaeological sites as numerous remains of settlements dating back to the late Bronze Age had been found. The recent discovery of a Roman villa dating back to the second century had also drawn attention to the park's rich historical heritage. Constable Collins pulled the car over near the main entrance and, through the baked window, Dylan could make out Sergeant Carter advancing towards him.

"Welcome Chief!" - David exclaimed, opening the door and trying, as best he could, to shield Dylan from the rain that was continuing to fall violently and relentlessly - "Unfortunately, there is no good news."

"Lisa Lawson?" - he asked as, huddled under the same umbrella, they walked briskly down the short stretch that separated them from the entrance to James Barry's Hospital.

"No, not Lisa... or rather, we may have some news that will turn the spotlight back on the Lawson case as well."

Before entering David closed his umbrella and set it down on the right side of the porch, then tapped his feet and realised that it had only taken a few seconds to completely soak his trousers to above the knees. Dylan, on the other hand, was inexplicably dry and no one would have thought he had been in that rain as the only clues were a few drops of water on the toe of his boots. Cursing the half-mouthed weather and the usual dumb luck of his friend, who obviously hadn't missed a chance to let slip a wry half-smile well aware of being noticed, David, with an annoyed gesture, signalled for him to follow.

"Area C." - he said.

"I'll take a guess. First floor and same ward where Lisa Lawson is admitted?" - Dylan retorted aloud.

David nodded - "Yeah, but this time Sally Smith is waiting for you."

Area C was one of five within the main structure, located to the left of the entrance and adjacent to area B, which was the central area and also housed the main entrance and reception. The various wards were divided between five large areas in the main structure and two other external buildings adjacent to it, Building F with one of the best psychiatric wards in all of London and Building G for infectious diseases. At a brisk pace the two of them disentangled themselves from the various corridors and reached, in less than two minutes, the entrance to the first floor of Aera C where, waiting for them, was agent Mark Thomas. Hospitals may be the cleanest places on earth but Dylan just couldn't stand that acrid smell of disinfectant constantly in the air.

Agent Thomas had been the first to intervene at the place where Sally Smith had been found and had never let her out of his sight until she had been laid down on the stretcher and entered the restricted area of the emergency room. Her face clearly showed signs of fatigue and she also looked pitiful, her uniform wet and muddy all over. Despite this she had done everything in her power and had been reassured that the girl would soon be taken to the ward and that she would be assigned to room C127, the very room where she was now accompanying Dylan and David.

The last time he had seen Lisa Lawson was in room 9 in corridor 4, number C149. The numbering of the rooms in James Barry's Hospital was very intuitive as the letter indicated the area or building, the first digit the floor, the second the corridor and the last identified the room.

"So, someone want to tell me what happened?" - Dylan asked impatiently and in a firm tone.

The time for waiting and guessing was over and it was time to get down to business. Constable Thomas introduced himself and, while signalling that he was being followed, began to set out the facts. They were on patrol on Hackbridge Road, he and fellow officer John Harris, who was currently busy filing a report at the station. They had just finished a short lunch break with the most classic of classics, some excellent Fish and Chips bought from a little place not far away on the London Road. They then turned onto

Hackbridge Road and headed for the fifth time in the day to the place where Lisa Lawson had been found six days earlier. They had since been advised to increase patrols in that particular area, not so much because they had any particular suspicions at the station, but more to appease the locals who had asked for more controls.

They were driving at a slow pace and, despite this, the windscreen wipers were struggling to sweep the water off the windscreen. Sudden gusts of wind made the car jerk and the pouring rain had significantly reduced visibility. They were advancing slowly and with their flashing lights on. They were on the east side of the River Wandle and were entering the bridge when Thomas was just in time to avoid the man who was literally throwing himself under their car waving his arms furiously. There was not a soul around and, up to that moment and despite the bad weather, the day was passing by peacefully. The man's appearance was like a flash in the sky.

"Well, maybe it doesn't quite fit as a comparison, but I really narrowly avoided him!" - continued Constable Thomas.

They pulled the car over and, in the pouring rain, followed the man who, continuing to make sweeping gestures for the two officers to follow him faster, passed through the green gate and headed briskly towards a large tree that stood right next to the stream. And it was there that they saw her. Sitting on the ground, her back resting against the tree, her head bowed and her hands dipped in the muddy grass, was a half-naked young girl. As they approached, they noticed that she was wearing what appeared to be a two-piece swimming costume or perhaps the latest fashionable underwear. On one shoulder was a small purple backpack, of the bag type, the kind usually used at the gym to store clothes and personal items. She appeared to be conscious, and as Agent Harris tried to cover her up using his jacket, Thomas radioed for help.

The girl did not seem to show any obvious signs of abuse but when Thomas tried to lift her head by gently resting his hand under her chin, she jerked it up and looking him steadily in the eyes hissed a call for help. That sudden gaze, at once blank and terrified, made the agent recoil and he lost his balance and fell heavily to the ground. The shock was so great that even now he was wondering what he had seen that was so terrible in those two heavenly eyes that, he would have bet anything, had made more than one boy fall in love before. When the ambulance arrived, Constable Thomas decided to climb aboard and accompany the girl to the hospital, while Constable Harris stayed behind to identify the man who had stopped them. He was a local resident who had just returned from work and was parking his car when he noticed the girl crawling on all fours on the lawn, half-naked, in the direction of the stream. He decided to chase her because the girl was not responding to his calls. She seemed to be in a trance and it was not easy for him to stop her and place her under that tree.

Inspector Dylan listened attentively and could not help but assess all the similarities with Lisa Lawson. But there were two big changes from the Lawson case: firstly, this girl had documents. In fact, during the short ride in the ambulance, Agent Thomas reported finding her papers in the outside pocket of the bag.

Sally Smith, English, twenty-two years old, domiciled in Romford - 'Very strange' - he thought.

She did not even have time to complete her thoughts that her gaze was drawn to the rapid movements of the nurses fumbling around the girl. He leaned over to get a better look and for the second time in less than an hour saw something that shocked him again. Sally Smith was motionless on the stretcher, her eyes fixed in the direction of the ambulance canopy, but she was furiously moving the fingers of her hands, which were completely bloody. The two nurses were struggling hard to remove the mud from the young woman's hands.

One of the two realised he had Agent Thomas' gaze on him, turned and said - "She no longer has most of her fingernails and some of her phalanges are worn to the bone. Now let's give her hands a cursory cleaning and splint her wrists so she doesn't keep scratching them on the gurney."

It was then that the officer noticed that the side of the stretcher facing him, at hand level, was covered with a mush of blood mixed with mud. At that exact moment, the image of the girl sitting under the tree with her arms at her sides and her hands sunk into the ground came back to him. He also remembered that stifled plea for help and became convinced that Sally was actually looking for someone to help her stop her hands.

"Poor thing, how much she was suffering, I didn't realise." - Agent Thomas finally said disconsolately, even though he was aware that he had done everything within his power.

"The fact that she is able to ask for help is a positive note, at least this girl will be able to help us understand what is going on." - David judged - "But I'm going to go to the bathroom now and dry off a bit and, officer, you'd better do that too otherwise you'll find yourself in bed tomorrow with a good bronchitis."

"Yes officer, we're here now, you may go." - said Dylan as, as usual, he began to confabulate to himself, walking back and forth between the walls of the corridor.

Four steps, turn, four more steps and another turn, something was bothering him but he still couldn't figure out what. He felt exactly like when you start holding the first pieces of a jigsaw puzzle but you don't know the final design imprinted on the box. His only certainty was that the Lawson case and the Smith case were linked and, if it was as he thought, they were in big trouble. He hoped he could at least keep the news out of the press, at least until it was too late to make it into the next day's papers.

Suddenly a squeak of all-too-worn wheels distracted him from his thoughts. There she was, Sally Smith, lying on a cot advancing inexorably towards him, both arms tied to the side of the bed and her hands fully bandaged. At first glance it looked as if the frantic movement of her fingers that Agent Thomas had described had stopped, but on closer inspection, as the cot reached his height, he could see that the muscles and tendons on her forearm were tense. That blank stare then was not so different from the one he had crossed all night trying to extract the slightest information from Lisa Lawson. Behind her passed in order a nurse pushing the cot, a lady in her fifties with reddened eyes who he later discovered was his mother and who had one hand resting on Sally's shoulder and finally Dr Anthony Green who, shaking his head, motioned him to wait outside the door.

Now he was certain. What awaited him was not good.

Nothing good

"Inspector...", Dylan roused himself again from his thoughts and turning around found himself face to face with Dr Anthony Green.

The two knew each other quite well although, until a week before, neither had ever known of the other's existence. But chance had put them on two accidental tracks and Lisa Lawson was the exact spot where they were supposed to meet along life's path. They had spent many hours together in the hope of solving a rebus where it was clear from the beginning that neither of them knew either the exact number of letters that made up the words or how many words the solution consisted of.

"Doctor, what's new?" urged Dylan.

The doctor walked in the direction of the vending machine just outside the corridor - "Let's get something hot, this time it's on me."

He inserted the coins into the machine's shiny slot and selected a lemon tea for Dylan, who he knew wasn't crazy about the vending machine's coffee and whom he described as a bland brown slop.

"One day I'll let you try a good espresso coffee!" - Dylan had promised him in one of the lulls of that long night they had spent together.

He, however, liked that bland slop and, as the dark liquid began to stain the glass, he said - 'Unfortunately, I have no good news'.

As impossible as it was to imagine, the Sally Smith case seemed to have all the makings of an even more tangled affair than that of Lisa Lawson. Starting with the girl's constant pleas for help.

'It's as if she is asleep with her eyes wide open, not aware of anything around her, as if imprisoned in a dream. Physical and psychic exhaustion combined with severe dysphonia is my first diagnosis." - and began nervously sipping his coffee.

Sally Smith had severe inflammation in her vocal cords, as if she had been screaming at the top of her lungs for an indefinite time and to the point of losing her voice.

"She keeps calling for help but, despite her best efforts, her voice is barely audible now."

"Agent Thomas was wrong" - Dylan thought aloud - "he thought the girl was asking him for help to stop her fingers from scratching the ground."

"Oh yeah, the fingers - I've never witnessed anything like that. What do you want me to say? No person could keep hurting themselves like that. By now they are in such a state that just touching them would cause unbearable pain. We have given her strong painkillers even though she doesn't seem to need them, and we have blocked her hands. All her fingers are splinted.".

There was nothing more to add and Dr Green suggested letting the night pass before trying to listen to the girl and possibly to her mother who would be of little help anyway. She had already reported to the emergency room that she had not seen her daughter since the morning when she went out and said she would be back in the evening and would eat out. It was the same story told by Lawson's parents, a daughter who leaves home in the morning promising to return in the evening. Dylan didn't think twice and took the advice, as he knew that he could trust the doctor with his life. And then he wouldn't spend another empty night in that blessed hospital!

"...what about Lisa Lawson? Do you have any news to tell me?" - Dylan asked as he scratched his forehead with his right hand - "I won't deny that I'm beginning to think the two cases are connected."

Anyone who knew him knew that when Dylan scratched his forehead it was a sign that he was pondering something.

"Two days ago we moved Lisa to Building F, to the psychiatric ward, so that more in-depth neuropsychological investigations could be carried out." - After taking a short pause he continued - "We are hydrating her intravenously since we still can't get her to drink fluids and her mouth continues to appear drier than the desert."

Then, with an expression somewhere between embarrassment and a sense of helplessness he added - "Confidence for confidence, we are also in a stalemate."

He took a further pause as if to reflect on the admission he had just made - "Remember, psychiatric ward. By tomorrow, however, Miss Smith will still be here.".

At that moment Sergeant Carter appeared, who had spent a good half hour in the bathroom trying to give his trousers a good drying using the hot jet of the electric towel.

"Hello Doctor" - he began with that hint of humour that rarely left him - "The trousers may not be perfect but at least my feet are dry. Any news?"

"Nothing good, David. We'll be back in the morning. My car is at the station, can you give me a lift home?"

"Certainly, it's nearly eight o'clock at night now and the pizza should be ready!"

"Then we're off Dr Green, see you tomorrow. Have a good night."

"Certainly" - with a defeated air, he bowed his head, turned and started walking in the direction of Miss Smith's room - "Good evening to you."

Eureka!

At last the clouds seemed to have exhausted their water supply and now the rain was falling lightly. They were almost home and even the wind had stopped. Dylan turned to his right to observe David who had gotten wet again and had been cursing incessantly, for at least five minutes, the man who had stolen his umbrella at the entrance to James Barry's Hospital. Obviously, these were the occasions not to be missed to throw petrol on the fire and Dylan knew well how to bait his friend to the point of exasperation. In fact, that tragicomic situation had served to put his mind back on the right track. Dylan had always promised himself that he would leave any work-related thoughts outside his front door, but this time he knew it would be quite hard. David, on the other hand, succeeded very well and, for that reason too, Dylan enjoyed his unwieldy company, which contributed in no small part to brightening up the evenings at the Walker household. For example, at that precise moment, as David pulled his car up as he entered the small yard in front of the house, he already knew what he was going to ask him. The car stopped, the engine turned off and, instead of opening the door, Dylan waited for David to turn towards him.

"You don't mind if I crash on the couch after pizza by any chance?" - he asked him, knowing full well that he never went home after evenings spent eating Sara's pizza and downing one can of beer after another - "I'm afraid we'll be tight."

Dylan smiled and as usual answered him - "No problem. It's not the first time and besides it's not like I'm sleeping with you on the sofa!"

"I was actually thinking of Jack Sparrow. Sara must surely have let him into the house in this weather."

And, as she said this, she opened the door and got out of the car, leaving Dylan speechless.

"Mom, Uncle David's here too! Yay!" - shouted the boys in chorus as Jack Sparrow pranced around all happy and left little flour footprints on the legs of the two.

Sara was super busy and, while with one eye she was checking the two pizzas already in the oven, she was busy seasoning the four others already ready and laid out on the table. A tornado seemed to have passed through the kitchen but, after such a day, for Dylan it was like having passed through the gate of heaven.

"Another bad day, isn't it?" - Sara asked

"To call it a bad day is a compliment." - David commented.

"Yeah... poor girl!"

"What do you mean, poor girl?" - asked Dylan in amazement.

The eight o'clock news had already broadcast the news, in an incomplete and confusing way as usual, and although no details had filtered out of the hospital, the usual experts had already gathered, all together, in the worst TV lounges, to comment and reason about the utter nothingness.

"Tomorrow there will be a competition again to publish the best headline." - he thought to himself, shaking his head - "and at the very least they'll demand my presence at the press conference too, damn them!"

Fortunately he now had something tastier to think about. The pizza was excellent as usual and, in order, they devoured a margherita with buffalo mozzarella, one with cooked ham and mushrooms, one with pepperoni, two frankfurters and fries which were the children's favourite and, finally, David's favourite, the quattro formaggi. Sara was a perfectionist and bought most of the ingredients in the best stocked Italian shop on the opposite side of central London. You could literally binge on her pizza, but thanks to the slow rising process, one of Sara's main prides, it was always easily digestible, so much so that David was always ready to mop up the evening leftovers at breakfast in the morning.

Those rare times there was something left over. The evening passed cheerfully, between one beer and another, with David, as always, untangling jokes and riddles.

"What is a fortuneteller to do who knows neither the present, nor the past, nor the future?"

The children enjoyed themselves like crazy trying to give the right answer, but the happiest child was always Uncle David because, often, no one could guess - "Learn the verbs better!" - and down with laughter.

"Speaking of verbs, how was your day at school?" - Dylan asked, turning to Janet, the eldest child of the Walker household who had recently turned eight.

"All good, Dad!" - she replied with a big smile.

"Yeah, everything's fine at school, a bit less so at home." - added one of the twins in a low voice with a sly, mischievous expression.

"Jack! You mind your own business! You always have to tell everything, huh?"

"Calm down guys, what could have happened that was so bad?" - Uncle David immediately tried to cool things down.

At that point Sara intervened and told how Janet, without asking her mother's permission, had taken the tablet to find some news about elephants that were the subject of a school research paper she had to prepare for the following week.

"You know you're not supposed to do that without mother's permission." - Dylan apostrophised her and added - "It's not even the first time it's happened, is it?"

"Yes, but she should have finally learned her lesson. This time the little one got scared because a video appeared among the first search results that she shouldn't have seen." - Sara added in annoyance.

"What video?" - asked Uncle David curiously as he bit into yet another piece of pizza.

"The video of that elephant in Sri Lanka trampling to death a man who appeared to be trying to hypnotise him." - he explained, electrocuting little Janet once again.

Dylan suddenly became serious. His mind began to race, he reasoned quickly and... - "No way, Sara you're a genius!" - he exclaimed so loudly that everyone started looking at him strangely.

A strange silence descended.

"Are you thinking what I'm thinking?" - he asked, turning sharply towards David with an expression that looked like the Syracusan inventor Archimedes about to shout 'Eureka!'.

"Um... what am I supposed to think, my friend?" - he mumbled with a full mouth, a thread of embarrassment and frowning.

"They've been hypnotised! Someone must have hypnotised them!"

A special mission

That morning Inspector Dylan Walker, contrary to his habits, got up very early. It was only 5.30 a.m. and the whole house was enveloped in an unusual silence. Normally he would have got up when the first cries of the boys came from the kitchen and Sara had been busy preparing breakfast for some time. The only thing he heard instead were the unmistakable ticking sounds coming from the stairs, which unmistakably unmasked the only living being in the house who, apart from him, was already awake. Jack Sparrow had not taken long to resume his old habit of speeding up and down the stairs.

"Sooner or later you're going to break your neck." - Dylan had repeatedly told him, but Jack, after each tumble, started running even faster than before.

"Hi Jack, I know you're still mad at me." - she passed him halfway up the stairs with her big dark eyes staring at him - "But there's no point looking at me like that anyway, your super kennel is out there waiting for you and as soon as everything is dry you're going back to your house."

He made to turn into the kitchen but changed his mind as soon as he heard David's blissful humming coming from the living room. He switched on the light - "Wake up boy, we have a busy day ahead of us today."

In reality, Dylan had slept little and badly because his thoughts had always been focused on that insight from the previous evening that could mark a turning point in the solution of the cases. David, on the other hand, was sunk on the sofa in the arms of Morpheus and waking him up at that hour would have been a feat.

"Desperate times call for desperate measures." - thought Dylan as he retrieved the small bottle of water that David always had on hand to quench his nocturnal thirst.

A sudden jet of water hit him full in the face - "What the fuck is going on?" - he yelled, waving his arms furiously and then wiping his eyes - "You got me all wet!"

In an irritated manner, slurring some new expletive, he got up from the couch, passed his friend without a glance and headed up the stairs, in the direction of the bathroom.

"After yesterday's rain you should be used to it." - Glissed Dylan as he resumed his way to the kitchen - "I'll turn on the espresso machine, a quick Italian breakfast and then let's get to work. You have three minutes, then I'll kick in the bathroom door."

A good ten minutes obviously passed before David joined him in the kitchen. Dylan had already finished his breakfast and David saw, on the side of the table, intended for him, a cup of espresso coffee, now lukewarm, some biscuits and a jar of berry jam.

"At noon I'm going to have to take out a bison." - he said half-mouthed as he took his seat at the table - "So, do you want to brief me on how we should go about this?"

Dylan had started walking nervously again, from one side of the kitchen to the other, his eyes fixed on his steps - "I'm now sure that the Lisa Lawson case and the Sally Smith case are connected in some way."

He walked over to the still lit coffee machine and began, as he did every morning, the preparation of his second coffee.

"And I'm not just referring to the possibility that they were both hypnotised. That will be my task to verify. Your job will be to scour their lives for anything that might relate one to the other." - And he began sipping his coffee - "This will be your special mission today.

Don't even show up at the station, go out and do everything you can to get any useful results."

He told them that he would have to follow up every lead, analyse their lives, their habits, especially talk to their parents. He should not only limit himself to gathering information, but should go as far as getting the girls' bedroom door opened as well.

"You mustn't miss a thing, and you take Mr and Mrs Smith's statement this time," he said.

"But Dylan, you know I'll need authorisation to do certain things." - Tempted David as he quietly observed the table that no longer offered anything to eat.

"I'm not joking and I don't have time to waste with procedures and authorisations. You know how to act in such cases. Make up a story that is credible, add a dash of hope and get everything you need. Don't forget all the access data to their social networks, email accounts and inspect their paper correspondence."

"Alright boss, I'll try to do what I can." - He gave a quick glance at the clock which barely read six o'clock - "I'll start at James Barry's Hospital where I'm sure I'll find someone to assist the two girls. I can't think of anything else I can do at this hour."

He got up and made his way out, not before patting the head of Jack Sparrow who had spent the whole time hunting for crumbs between the table legs.

"Ah, David... let me know as soon as you have any news, and if you don't, know that I won't want to see you until you find it."

"Say hi to the kids and give Sara a hug. Thank her for the pizza." - He made to close behind the door, then opened it again and added with a wide smile - "You know you can trust me, I'll see you at dinner!"

Dylan returned the smile, then, through the window, followed his friend as he climbed into his new Jeep Renegade, strictly black, like every other car he'd ever owned in his life. It was still pitch black outside and, from the way David was moving, it must have been pretty cold too. The car backed up and then disappeared down Longfield Avenue. Those were the moments when she thanked God that she had put that lump of David in her life.

Seeking confirmation

Dylan had already decided that the first thing to do was to prove to himself that his intuition had a possible basis in truth. He did not know much about hypnosis. Even during his studies he had dealt with the subject in a very marginal way and his only memories were of that fake hypnotist, whose name he could hardly remember at the moment, who, when he was a child, used to jump from broadcast to broadcast pretending to hypnotise the unfortunate guests, who were forced to make a very bad impression in order to humour him. He turned on his laptop and started reading everything the search engine returned about hypnotism, techniques, potential and real cases documented on the net. About two hours passed and, as the house came to life, he was still hunched over the computer, only taking his eyes off the monitor when he was tapping on the keyboard or taking notes. Sara's arrival woke him up.

"Good morning dear, have you been up long?" - his wife greeted him, planting a kiss on his forehead as she moved his hair with one hand - "There, now it's perfect!"

Dylan's hair was black, short and so curly that a couple of quick movements with his hands were enough to get it into place. The children had also woken up and one could clearly discern the first squabbles of the morning as they descended the stairs.

"Man, it's already eight o'clock!" - He returned the kiss and, as he closed his laptop, hailed a taxi - "I'll see you for dinner, David will be there."

Sara shrugged - "They say that where there's for five, there's also for six... but if the sixth eats for three what about that?"

"Five plus three is eight, and with Jack Sparrow it's nine!" - promptly inserted Janet, who was making her entrance into the kitchen as the leader of the little train of little ones in the Walker household.

She was a very intelligent child, passionate about numbers and a lover of mathematics. At eight years old, she could solve operations in her head that, for her age, should have been very complex. Dylan hugged and kissed them one by one, then took his long black coat from the coat rack on the wall near the front door, the ever-present black leather briefcase with all his paperwork, and greeted everyone with a smile - "Be good, mind you!"

He closed the door behind him and was happy to see that the taxi was already on the street waiting for him. The rain had finally given way to a warm sunshine and, on the drive to James Barry's Hospital, Dylan carefully re-read the notes he had taken. In those two hours he had discovered that a subject under hypnosis can be involved not only in the psychological dimension but also in the physical one. The fact that a hypnotist could influence both the psychophysical condition and the behavioural conditions of a subject was the part that most caught his attention. There was thus a real possibility of intervening in a person's mind by altering their perception of the outside world. According to what he had read, a subject in that particular state of hypnosis could not only fail to perceive real external stimuli but also perceive stimuli that existed only in his mind. Another article dealt with the possibility of being able to control voluntary musculature and to a certain extent suppress pain. As he read it, he was reminded of the words of Dr Anthony Green, who could not understand how Sally Smith could continue to hurt herself, despite being in a state where any human being would find what she was doing unbearable. That's why he was going back to James Barry's Hospital, to talk to Dr Green himself, in the hope that at least he wouldn't take him for a fool and that, above all, he could help him out. He had already warned Chief

Inspector Cooper that he would probably be out for the day. Martin Cooper had literally bombarded him with constant text messages, asking him to take that hot potato off his hands as soon as possible. The boss didn't think twice about giving him carte blanche and maximum freedom of action, as long as he solved the damn cases as quickly as possible. Dylan had hinted to him that he had a lead to follow but, even though he had been urged to say more, he had avoided saying anything more because, knowing Cooper, he would have taken him for a fool.

He could already imagine him complaining loudly in the corridors of the police station - "A madman dealing with madmen, that's who that Inspector Walker is!".

The more he thought about it the more convinced he was that he had made the right choice in keeping quiet.

"That'll be £9."

The taxi driver's voice snapped him out of his thoughts. He quickly settled the bill, opened the door and, at the sight of the hospital entrance, he thought how it was already the third time in seven days that he had been there. First Lisa Lawson, then Sally Smith, at least today there was no one waiting for him, apart from four journalists near the entrance whom he managed to avoid without making any statements.

"Good morning, could you please tell me where I can find Dr. Anthony Green?" - he asked at the reception desk.

A lady in her fifties, without looking up from her paperwork, rearranged her glasses and replied - "It depends...".

"And what does it depend on?"

"Well, on who wishes to meet him..." - he did not have time to finish the sentence that, halfway between his glasses and the paperwork, as if by magic, a service badge from the Southern Police District of London appeared.

"Yes, I admit I'm photogenic but, if you prefer, you can also look up and get a better look at me in person." - Dylan urged, sketching a smile.

With cheeks redder than two San Marzano tomatoes, the very ones Sara used on her pizzas, the receptionist picked up a large register, flipped through a couple of pages and made an internal call.

"Everyone has a bad day." - Dylan thought to himself as the lady fumbled nervously with her glasses.

He always maintained an unusual calm at such times as he knew that behind a rude reply or a provocative gesture there was always a person who might be at a not too happy moment in their life.

On a first reading 'Psychocybernetics' by Maxwell Maltz had seemed to him a heavy book like a brick but he recognised that it contained some really interesting insights that had changed his approach to everyday life.

"Dr Green hasn't arrived yet but he should be here any minute. I was told he is expected at nine o'clock in psychiatry. Do you know where he is?" - he asked in the best polite tone he could muster at that moment.

Dylan shook his head but remembered that Dr. Green had alerted him to the fact that Lisa Lawson had been transferred there.

"Building F, outside this facility. Follow the central corridor, then take a left and go through all areas C, D and E. Find Building F at the exit, on the other side of the street." - and with a triumphant air he concluded - "Psychiatry, the studies are on the first floor, the patients on the second. There's also a third floor but you're unlikely to find anyone there.".

Satisfied with how she had handled the situation, she put on her glasses again and bent over her paperwork.

From dusk to dawn

That lady leaning weakly against the doorframe, and with a face that tells the story of someone who has not seen a good bed and proper rest for too long, must have been Lisa's mother. She had never met her as she had arrived at the hospital in the early hours of the previous Saturday morning, shortly after the time Dylan had left her. The task of listening to Lisa Lawson's parents was given to a couple of police officers who were on duty the next day in the area of James Barry's Hospital. At the time it felt like a strange case, but certainly not to that extent, so Chief Inspector Cooper had preferred not to disturb Dylan any further and leave David to do some important paperwork in the office. Mrs Lawson had her gaze firmly fixed in the direction of her daughter, the girl who, for nothing in the world, would have let a day go by without cuddling her. Instead she was now there, motionless, sitting on the edge of the bed staring at a wall that was about two metres from her nose. Reaching the doorway, Dylan could now see her too, against the light as Lisa had a large window behind her through which a few warm rays of sunlight were streaming in. Her long red hair was pulled back into a braid that went down her right shoulder, a cherry-coloured dressing gown that emphasised her fair skin even more, while from her left sleeve came the small tube leading to an IV. He immediately recognised that blank stare he had already met for too long and which had haunted him for at least a couple of nights.

"Good morning" - there he was again lost in thought - "Are you looking for someone?"

"Good morning, sorry, I didn't mean to disturb you. I'm Inspector Walker, Dylan Walker." - He introduced himself, extending his hand to her.

Mrs Lawson's face lit up - "Inspector Walker! You don't know how pleased I am to be able to meet you. I'm Clare Lawson, Lisa's mother."

Dylan was somewhat surprised at how he was greeted by Clare, who did not stop shaking his hand tightly - "The pleasure is mine Mrs Lawson."

"Just call me Clare. What's new?" - he asked impatiently.

"Just some ideas for now. I have come to meet Dr Anthony Green. Right now you only think about being close to your daughter." - Dylan tried to put a stop to the conversation that was already making him uncomfortable.

"Come on, you can talk to me, Inspector. I had a conversation until a few minutes ago with Sergeant Carter, who told me that you are close to solving the case. Did you hear about the other girl? Lisa and Sally don't deserve this situation."

"Fuck! A pinch of hope David, I said give just a pinch of hope!" - Dylan mumbled to himself.

As luck would have it, at that very moment, the unmistakable silhouette of Dr Green materialised from down the hall. American, originally from Boston, 39 years old, a couple of inches taller than Dylan, with jet-black hair, Anthony Green walked with a slight limp from a motorbike accident some twenty years ago. He was on the Massachusset Turnpike, returning from Fenway Park where he had just attended a Boston Red Sox game, when he was run over by a truck that had failed to notice the slowdown due to construction work. He called himself a miracle worker and it was then that he decided that his purpose in life would be to care for others, just as the doctors at Massachusetts General Hospital had done for him. He candidly admitted that coming from a wealthy family was an advantage for his career as, after passing the tough entrance tests, he easily managed to pay for his studies at the

University of Harward, Cambridge. After graduating from medical school, he moved to London, where he brought all his enthusiasm, his desire to be a point of reference for the sick and also the ever-present red socks he wore in any situation. He had always been fascinated by the possibility of being able to explore places and cultures other than those in the United States and, although he did not find soccer as interesting as baseball, he was delighted to accept the offer from James Barry's Hospital, a highly professional facility to which he had applied five years earlier. He and Dylan had had plenty of time to get to know each other during their time at Lisa Lawson's bedside.

"Dr. Green, I've been looking for you." - Dylan exclaimed loudly, walking up to him at a brisk pace to put maximum distance between him and Mrs Lawson, then added in a lower but firm voice - "You really need to give me a few minutes. Away from here!"

Dr Green blinked and then materialised a knowing smile, turning in Mrs Lawson's direction - "Good morning Clare, have you noticed any improvement or anything different from yesterday overnight?"

"Unfortunately not, Lisa continues to stare at the wall without uttering a word." - And she seethed as she leaned back against one of the side jambs of the door.

Dr Green entered the room followed like a shadow by Dylan, pulled a firefly out of his right pocket and started pointing the thin beam of light, passing from one eye to the other of Lisa. The girl had no reaction. Meanwhile Dylan leaned against the wall and with his right hand began to scratch his forehead, trying to work out what signal his sixth sense was sending him at that precise moment. Even the neurological gavel continued to give no results and, despite the stimuli, Lisa showed no reflex response. He had already been enlightened by Dr. Green on the need for such tests, which served as a quick check to measure the integrity of the patient's neural network. Then, like a sudden flash in the darkest sky, Dylan had an insight that would even make Shakti Gawain proud. He had always been fascinated by the writings of one of the most famous New Age authors, a pioneer in the field of personal growth, psychological self-help and the development of awareness and self-esteem. He got to know her through her most successful book, "Creative Visualisations", but Dylan had been bewitched by "The Power of Intuition", which had literally helped him recover that great capacity for intuition that, according to the author, everyone has at birth but which, with the passage of time, tends to fade until it disappears altogether. He had read that book more than once and, whenever he had an epiphany, he thought - "Man, this really works!".

And this time was no different. In fact it was much better, because this insight was a further point in favour of his thesis that that girl who was sitting in front of him was in a state of hypnosis.

"Doctor... Clare... am I mistaken or is Lisa staring at the wall whereas, when she was admitted to the old ward, she constantly stared at the window?" - He interrupted the silence in the room.

"No, she's not wrong." - Clare replied.

"Has she ever looked out of the window since she was brought here?" - Dylan urged.

"I can assure you that she has always had her eyes fixed in the direction of that damn wall." - Clare pointed out, showing a thread of nervousness for the first time.

In truth, after many sleepless nights, she was still far too lucid and calm. Dr Green listened attentively. He too had noticed this strangeness but had never given it much thought - "What are you thinking, Inspector?" - he asked curiously.

Dylan took a few seconds to pause and then said - "I don't have a great sense of direction but the rays of the rising sun are coming in through this window while in the old room the sun was setting in the direction of the window. So, in my opinion, Lisa is continuing to look in exactly the same direction as before.".

Mrs Lawson, of course, did not see how this would help in finding a solution, but Dr Green immediately sprang to his feet, putting both the gavel and the firefly back in his pocket.

"Clare, for now I too don't notice any improvement but rest assured that with the specialist care in this department we will begin to see it in short order." - Dr Green wouldn't have bet a pound on what he had just said but he knew it was important to always give positive expectations - "Inspector, I'd love to have a word with you. Can you follow me into the study?"

He didn't even wait for an answer, which would have been irrelevant anyway, and, waving goodbye to Mrs Lawson, he left the room and began, with his classic limping gait, striding down the corridor, with Dylan following three steps behind him. They went down one floor and Dr Green, contrary to what he had said, headed for the bar, taking a seat at the table furthest from the counter. He made a quick gesture with his hand in the direction of one of the barmaids who was standing near the till at that moment, then settled back in his chair and leaned towards Dylan with his elbows resting on the table and his chin resting on his hands. It really was a nice bar, bright, with new furnishings, a high standard of cleanliness and above all Dylan appreciated that, at last, the smell of the food and hot drinks had replaced that pungent smell of disinfectant that he just couldn't get used to.

"Go Dylan, I'm all ears." - Dr Green exclaimed in a finally informal manner.

He didn't know if he was more afraid of being taken for a fool or of having his hypothesis irretrievably rejected, but Dylan didn't let it be repeated twice and replied flatly - "I think Lisa and Sally have been hypnotised. Anthony Green did not flinch and invited them to continue with a brief wave of his hand. It was then that Dylan finally got rid of everything in his mind and, like a river in flood, told how he had had that intuition and how he had then tried to connect the various pieces of the puzzle.

"Sally who would keep ruining her fingers without feeling the slightest pain, the absence of reflexes, Lisa's fixed gaze pointed in one direction" - he began to list everything that could support his thesis by rummaging through his notes - "and that feeling that they are living in a virtual reality, a sort of parallel life... Anthony, what do you think?"

He was well aware that his hypothesis was a stretch but he had no other way to go, at least for the time being. Exposing himself to Dr Green in this way, although he trusted him, was certainly a gamble, but he had decided it was worth the risk. At that moment the barmaid arrived at the table with a small bottle of water and two glasses - "Your usual water Dr Green."

"Thank you Elaine."

Antony, who had been listening attentively up to this point, gave thanks and took the opportunity to take a further moment of reflection. He opened the bottle, poured the water into the two glasses, handed one of them to Dylan and brought his own to his mouth. Then he cleared his throat.

"Dylan, what do you want me to think?" - he paused for another long moment - "As a doctor I think you have hastily come to an absolutely wrong conclusion. There is nothing scientific to back up your fanciful hypothesis."

Dylan took the blow and dejectedly leaned heavily on the backrest, letting his arms fall to his sides. The last two weeks had been anything but easy, no real break from work and sleepless nights spent visualising the moment when he would solve that case. He confidently believed in creative visualisation, which he had approached by reading Bob Proctor's writings, but this time it seemed to him that he had drawn a blank, his servo-mechanism had led him astray. They spent a few interminable seconds staring into each other's eyes and then Dr Green added: "If I was out of here, without this doctor's coat, maybe taking a nice jog in Beddington Park, I could tell you how your intuition is quite fascinating and I could also give you the reference of a person who might be right for you. Or rather our case." Those few words were enough to make Dylan snap back into his chair, straight as a die - "I see nothing but green meadows, trees and blue waters around us." - he said with the look of someone who had just realised he had made a Condor, 'hole in one', on a PAR 5 hole.

Finally Dr Green also showed his excitement at the idea that Dylan had been right and was already looking forward to the phone call he would be making shortly.

Anthony was well aware that there were a number of experienced hypnotherapists in the UK, some of them very good and famous, with important achievements behind them, all members of nationally recognised professional associations.

But it was not them he was thinking of at that moment.

There is no needle in the haystack

Perhaps she had exaggerated a bit but initially Mrs Lawson had not seemed as accommodating as she had hoped. In fact, she had already told the police everything she remembered and, noting the lack of progress in the investigation and her daughter's stationary condition that showed no signs of improvement, she had no desire to stand there repeating everything that was already on the record. She was clearly tired and so the only way she could wring some new information out of her was to tell her that there was finally a very good lead to follow up and that the situation would soon be resolved.

'I just hope that Dylan doesn't meet Clare Lawson, at least in the next ten days'. - thought David as he entered the roundabout between Hackbridge Road and London Road, heading for the Lawson's house.

Waiting for him was Clare's husband to whom his wife had given very specific instructions over the phone, warning him to comply with any request Sergeant Carter made of him. At James Barry's Hospital, David got nothing more than what he already knew and Mrs Lawson only despaired of being able to protect her little girl. Her words of comfort were of no avail in explaining that at the age of twenty-one, one is no longer a child and that, at that age, one cannot fully control the lives of children.

"She may have unintentionally witnessed something that shocked her or she may have had contact with untrustworthy people. You know how young people are, they get up to all sorts of things." - said with great conviction and nonchalance the man who knew exactly what he was talking about.

"Sergeant Carter, I can categorically rule out the possibility that my Lisa hung out with untrustworthy people. My little girl would never have done such a thing without informing me. Her father and I are her whole life, she would never wrong us like that.".

As he drove north along the London Road, David couldn't help but think how lucky he had been not to grow up under a bell jar - "Lisa has as much chance of survival within society as a gazelle, born in captivity and then released on the savannah in front of a herd of lions on a month-long diet, would have." - he thought. In the meantime he had reached his destination and parked the car as best he could, with two wheels on the pavement. Mr Robert Lawson, who was already waiting for him at the door, introduced himself, showed him in and escorted him upstairs, directly to Lisa's room. He, too, did not look well.

When he reached the second door to the right of the stairs, he stopped and opened it - "If you need anything, call me." - and after a short pause - "I'll wait for you downstairs." - he finally added in a resigned tone, making David sit down and closing the door behind him.

The room was in semi-darkness and the first thing David noticed was how tidy and carefully stored everything was. He ran a finger over a shelf to the left of the door and found no trace of dust. After switching on the light, he took a quick look inside the wardrobe, at the two drawers on either side of the bed and then decided to focus on the small white desk to the right of the half-closed window, on which a laptop computer was resting. He began to check what the middle drawer contained, even though he felt he was uncomfortable rummaging through a woman's belongings. He had never been good with the fairer sex but of one thing he was certain and it was right there before his eyes.

"All girls have their own secret diary." - he told himself visibly pleased with the discovery.

While waiting for the laptop to turn on, he took pictures of the diary pages and then neatly put everything back in its place. Even though he had already found the diary page where she had transcribed all the passwords to her social networks, her email service and the various sites where she had signed up, he was relieved to find everything already stored. He spent about two hours going through everything he could find in the girl's last month of online activity and filled pages and pages of notes. David was not an IT expert but it was obvious that there was nothing particularly interesting there that he needed to bother a specialist with at the moment. In fact, he found only a lot of teaching material and the usual things that might interest a girl such as fitness, fashion, gossip and a few cute boys. He therefore decided to move on as it was now eleven o'clock and he had a long journey ahead of him in the direction of Romford. The appointment with the housekeeper of the Smith house was for 1.30 p.m. and, if all went well, he would arrive early, with the possibility of stopping to get something to eat. Sally Smith's parents, both present at the hospital that morning, unlike Mrs Lawson, had been happy to talk to him. They did not even object to his request to have a look around the house among their daughter's belongings and immediately alerted their maid to wait for him at home. However, he had to see that even the conversation with Annie and Nathan Smith was not very helpful, as there was nothing abnormal in the poor girl's life. He therefore hoped to find something interesting in this last attempt of the day. David said goodbye to Mr Lawson and, as he was on his way again, called the station. In that situation they should have left no stone unturned. He instructed the responding officer to call upstairs and request the requisition of all surveillance camera footage in the area of the bridge over the River Wandle, from the intersection of Nightingale Road and Dale Park Avenue to the west, to all within a hundred and fifty metre radius to the east of the bridge. He also requested an analysis of the two girls' phone records and inquired about the status of the location of the smartphones, as both devices had not yet been recovered. Agent Patel, whom he knew very well, informed him that they were doing everything possible to get answers quickly.

Before ending the conversation came the usual question - "Sergeant Carter, you did not come by the station today. How is your special mission going?"

"Bad Archie, very bad. Worse than finding a needle in a haystack.".

Professor Benjamin Hunt

It was just after eleven thirty and, while David, hungry as a bear just awakened from hibernation, was on his way to Romford, on the other side of the ocean Professor Benjamin Hunt was taking his classic morning jog at Old Morse Park in Cambridge. It was shaping up to be a beautiful day, but the cold, at seven thirty in the morning, was still making itself felt. This was certainly not a problem for Benjamin, who had kept up that habit since he was a boy, displaying a physical fitness to make all those twenty-somethings who now spend their time hopping from one sandwich shop to another envious. In his early forties, he was one of the youngest professors with a chair at Harvard Medical School. His teaching was based on the effectiveness of the learning method called Problem Based Learning. P.B.L. was a classical model of problem-based learning whereby it was established that complex real-world situations, which have no right answer, are the basis of learning and that, moreover, problems themselves lead to the development of clinical problem-solving skills.

That morning his jog was interrupted by the ringing of his smartphone. He slowed down his run and started walking slowly, catching his breath, then picked up his mobile phone and watched curiously as Anthony Green's name lit up on the screen. It had been at least ten years since they had seen each other but he still remembered well the afternoons spent as youngsters in the stands cheering on the Red Sox and the intense days spent studying at Harvard.

"Anthony! What fair wind?" - he exclaimed in a tone that hinted at a deep happiness at hearing from his great friend who had flown to make a career in the old world. It was the first time Dr Green had called the United States at that hour, as he used to phone when it was already lunchtime in Boston and he was sure to find his parents at home. He did this once every two days since he had first moved to London. That morning, however, he knew he would find Benjamin already wide awake running around in some Cambridge park as he was not the kind of person to give up his habits easily. They spent the first five minutes chatting and joking as if they had not seen each other since the previous evening, then Anthony got to the point. He briefly told him the facts and emphasised the fact that they were analysing two cases, at first sight without solution, and the possibility that they were facing particular plastic manifestations of the creative imagination due to unknown hypnotic techniques. For Dylan what Dr Green was saying on the phone was as clear as Arabic and he marvelled at how comfortable Anthony seemed to be in that field.

"You know very well why I am asking for your help and we urgently need you to join us here in London." - Dr Green concluded.

Professor Hunt stopped for a while in the middle of the path he was on. It was not so much the request to leave for London immediately that surprised him as the hint that he might have to investigate suspected cases of hypnosis. After all, Anthony was one of the few people who knew of his deep interest in hypnotism and his mastery of its techniques. His passion was a kind of parallel life that, in conjunction with his medical studies, he had always pursued with continuous training on the subject that had fascinated him since he was a boy. He had never wanted to regularise his skills, he had no recognised professionalism and those who knew about it could be counted on the tip of one hand, despite the fact that over time he had secretly applied the techniques he had learnt more than once and always with excellent results. Good Anthony had offered to be his guinea pig more than once. Sometimes he felt like a new Galileo Galilei and, before making his studies known, he would continue to test his intuitions until he had all the results to support his ideas. He had always been convinced that many complex and at first sight inexplicable situations could be solved by applying correct hypnosis techniques. Of course the two cases Anthony had described to him were quite strange and far beyond his wildest imagination, but it was precisely this that made him immediately accept his friend's request. As soon as the conversation was over, Anthony gave the good news to Dylan who was waiting impatiently - "Tomorrow, Professor Benjamin Hunt will be here in London. He will give me confirmation of his arrival time later on. He has to both check his flights and figure out how to get a few days away from classes.".

Dylan suddenly felt relaxed, everything had gone as he had imagined and, without applying any force, he had relied on what circumstances had put in front of him. He realised that he had leaned back and was also particularly tired - "I think it's time to put something in my teeth." - he said and with a smile added - "Sergeant Carter must be starving."

As they walked towards the restaurant she told him about her relationship with David and how she had sent him out that morning in search of further clues.

"I wonder if he found anything interesting?" - he thought - "I'll certainly have to make it up to him at dinner. I was a bit too harsh on him this morning.". With that in mind he called home to warn Sara, who would certainly be able to cope.

"Lasagna, beer chicken, baked sausages with potatoes, salad and a couple of good bottles of red wine. Would that do?" - She knew Sergeant Carter's tastes all too well to be wrong.

After all, it was she who had been the cause of the sudden change in David's dietary regime, which had quickly fallen into line with the habits of the Walker household, where dinner was the largest meal of the day and one never started eating before twenty-thirty. Before then he used to stop to eat outside the house for a classic

Fish and Chips or, every other day, he went to his mother's house, where a single dish awaited him, which could be roast beef with vegetables or cornish pasties, a meat and vegetable pie, baked and wrapped in puff pastry. David had immediately enjoyed the convivial atmosphere at the Walker home when everyone, sitting around a table overflowing with food, recounted the events of the day and put their daily problems behind them. After a light lunch, Dylan said goodbye to Dr. Green and decided it was time to make a trip to the station. He remembered that he had to retrieve the car he had left the previous day and he would also have to report to Chief Inspector Cooper, who was frantic for news. After the latest rumours that the very existence of S.I.P. was in the balance, Martin Cooper was aware that this could be the right opportunity to prove both the usefulness of his team and his ability to handle a rather complex situation. The S.I.P. had spent a difficult morning on the phone with the main newspaper editors to keep a low profile in their news reports and not exasperate a situation that was beginning to worry them. He was very frank with them, expressing his concern, and promised them that they would be notified promptly if there was any news.

"Congratulations boss, I can confirm that when I left James Barry's Hospital there was no journalist there except for a camera crew who were probably recording a report for the news." - Dylan was very relieved not to have to worry too much about the press. At least for a few days. He knew how important information was but also how damaging it could be in certain circumstances. He thought that this day, in spite of everything, had been a good one as he would return home with some more hope, one less thought and the certainty that David would give him more good news. Unfortunately for him, this last conviction was shattered as soon as he returned home and saw David slumped on the sofa in the living room with a tired and disconsolate expression. Dylan returned home that it was about seven thirty in the evening and a rainbow of smells was already coming from the kitchen. He found Sara, as usual, busy at the cooker, Janet helping her mother set the table, and the twins still in their room who, from the noises coming from upstairs, were certainly racing the toy car track they had found under the tree on Christmas Day. He put his coat on the coat rack and, after the usual exchange of long hugs with the princess of the house, a kiss to Sara and a nod to David, headed upstairs to say goodbye to the little Walkers and above all to take a rejuvenating shower. David, on the other hand, continued reading and re-reading the notes he had taken, looking at the photos in his smartphone and trying to find some point of contact between the two girls. The dinner was nothing short of superlative, spent in full merriment, between David's usual riddles, the boys' fat laughs and Sara who, as usual, was entertaining any conversation that could be a valid distraction from the busy day. The two friends understood each other on the fly and would catch up after dinner, as soon as the boys had gone to bed. In the middle of dinner, however, Dylan had received the expected news, a text message from Dr. Green advising him that Professor Hunt would be arriving the next day, at noon, at London Heathrow airport, terminal number 4. In response, he confirmed their willingness to pick him up on arrival. As soon as the little ones had gone to sleep Dylan and David were alone in the living room, with Sara busy tidying up the kitchen.

"Listen David, we have a long day of work tomorrow too. At noon we have an appointment at Heathrow airport. I'd say it's time to get some rest. We'll catch up in the morning on the hour or so drive to the airport." - Said Dylan with a consoling pat on his friend's shoulder - "And I think you also need to get home, have a nice shower and get some sleep in a comfortable bed."

"What time shall I pick you up boss?" - David replied rather relieved. One of the qualities he had always appreciated about Dylan was that he always knew when a point needed to be made. And that evening was definitely one of those times.

"Calmly, I'll see you at ten o'clock. On the dot."

Well done David!

This was not going to be an ordinary Sunday. Dylan felt it and was excited at the idea that he would soon be able to get some crucial answers that would shed more light on the Lawson and Smith cases. Despite everything, he had managed to sleep until eight o'clock and got up in perfect shape. Actually, he would have slept a little longer but, like every Sunday morning, the twins had wasted no time in jumping on his bed. But it was only fair. He would probably spend that Sunday away from home and so it was only right to at least enjoy a long breakfast with his family. David showed up ten minutes early and waited for Dylan's arrival by staying in the car. He had left his car at the station and had taken an official car as he might need to park in the reserved spaces near the Terminal 4 exit in the southern part of the airport. They had about an hour's journey ahead of them and used it to review the events of the previous day. David had a strange look on his face and still seemed to be particularly tired.

"You didn't go through your beer reserves once you got home, did you?" - Dylan apostrophised him - "I begged you to rest because today was going to be a busy day."

David looked at him slantingly, with a serious expression. Then he hinted a smile.

"You're right, I didn't get much sleep last night but, unfortunately, my fridge is more deserted than the Sahara desert." - David replied, thinking that maybe he should have tidied up a bit in what was once a nice house while now it seemed to be more messy than an open-air dump.

"I'll admit that last night I didn't hold out much hope of finding a connection between the two girls and I think you understood that since you didn't ask me anything." - he paused briefly - "But what you couldn't have known is that I still had one last thing to do. Not that I had high hopes, mind you."

David recounted how, at first glance, even the visit to the Smith house had turned out to be a bust. Sally and Lisa, different characters and upbringings, basically had the normal interests that girls at that age have such as fashion, physical activity and handsome boys. Nothing in particular caught her attention. On the way back to Hackbridge, the only faint hope lay in Sally Smith's laptop computer that she had taken with her. The history of sites visited had revealed nothing abnormal, but he had been unable to find the credentials to access social networks or email services. He had thought about referring him to a computer expert but perhaps he had another card to play and decided he would return to James Barry's Hospital the next day to talk to the Smiths. He was well aware that one of the biggest lapses young people make is to write down, somewhere, the login details, username and password, of the various sites that require registration. Only, unlike with Lisa, Sally had left no trace of them, at least not in her room. He hoped, therefore, that his parents had been able to help him retrieve them. He would need a stroke of luck and it was, just as he was on his way home, that he remembered how they had found the girl's papers inside the bag on the day she was found. A quick call to the station was all he needed to confirm that, among the various personal effects, a T-shirt, trousers and a pair of tennis shoes, there was also a small bottle of water, the house keys, a small torch that served as a key ring and an agenda.

"Bingo!" - he turned to Dylan who was now listening to him without uttering a word.

"I spent most of the night rummaging through that poor girl's life but finally managed to find a faint connection between the two." - announced David with satisfaction - "It could be mere coincidence but both Sally and Lisa visited the Roman London Museum in St Helier in early February."

David explained how he'd been drawn to a particular photograph they'd both posted on their Instagram profiles, showing them standing alongside what appeared to be a Roman-era half-bust. The all-too-close publication dates of two February for Sally and three February for Lisa convinced him that it could be more than just a coincidence.

"You can't be sure that the publication dates coincide exactly with the day of the visit but it is an interesting circumstance nonetheless." - Admitted Dylan - "Well done David and sorry about carlier but...".

"Don't worry Dylan, we're all a bit tired and anyway, if I'd had a small beer in the fridge I'd certainly have taken it out!" - David sneeringly interrupted him - "What about you?".

The rest of the trip passed with Dylan telling of his meeting with Anthony and Professor Hunt who they were on their way to pick up at the airport. He was relieved and delighted to hear that Dylan had found some concrete help, not least because someone like Dr Green would never have bothered so much if he had not found his hypothesis more than plausible. Flashing his lights, David pulled up right in front of the exit to Terminal 4. It was almost noon but they would certainly have to wait a good half hour for all the paperwork to be completed for non-EU citizens setting foot on British soil. The controls were strict and although they caused delays, no one complained as there was an atmosphere of absolute security. Not least Heathrow, according to the latest surveys, was the busiest airport in Europe and the one through which more international passengers passed than any other airport in the world. Dylan knew that Professor Hunt would have to go through the red exit as he was carrying what he described in a message as his bag of 'tools of the trade' and would therefore have to declare it on arrival. And there they were, Dylan intent on reading the latest news in The Sun and David evidently uncomfortable with the sign in his hand reading 'Professor Hunt', when Benjamin Hunt stopped in front of them. Five foot eight inches, short hair already greying, glasses, a lean physique, he had both hands full, on one side a red trolley bag and on the right a hard black briefcase.

"Here we are." - he began, smiling - "Benjamin Hunt to serve you." - He said, addressing Dylan directly.

"I assume you recognised Inspector Walker because of the two he is the only one without a sign." - David inserted himself, sketching a smile before Dylan was able to respond to the greeting.

On those occasions David was exceptional at breaking the ice and that hint of normal awkwardness that exists when two people meet for the first time.

"If you could use your tongue in this way even with the fairer sex by now you wouldn't be standing here at Heathrow between two men far taller than you!" - immediately pressed Dylan and then extended his hand towards Professor Hunt - "It is indeed a pleasure to meet you Professor Hunt, welcome. You can just call me Dylan and this subject to my left, Sergeant Carter, is my trusted friend David."

"Thank you Dylan, thank you David for the nice welcome. I am Benjamin Hunt but you can call me simply Benji."

"Ah, Benji... like Benjamin Price the unbeatable goalie from the Holly and Benji series!" - David couldn't resist the temptation to unleash all his Japanese cartoon culture.

"Yeah sure, just like him!" - Professor Hunt laughingly confirmed.

Positive feelings

Dr Green sat alone at a table set for four people, so large that it could have accommodated at least as many. In the morning he had requested that a large table be reserved for him at the restaurant on the first floor of Building F for 2pm, when he would be joined by three other people for a working lunch. Anthony had spent the last few hours trying to detect any kind of anomalies the two girls might manifest to further support Dylan's intuition. For example, such as the one found in Sally Smith who kept moving her lips exactly as she had been doing since the day she arrived at the hospital, when she could still faintly call for help. Initially, they had thought it was an inflammation of the vocal cords caused by exertion, but subsequent checks in the following days not only ruled out the possibility that the situation had worsened, but even found an unexpected improvement. But it was another sensational discovery that left him bewildered that day, especially as he could not explain it medically at all. He had been thinking about it since mid-morning, but it was now 2.30 p.m. and, sitting at the table, he kept turning and turning the pencil between his fingers, waiting for an epiphany that was late in coming.

"Maybe I'd better take this coat off this time." - he thought to himself.

Contrary to his duties, he had in fact made the decision not to reveal to any colleague what he had just discovered - "I'll wait to intervene further on Lisa and Sally, or at least I won't do so until I've heard Benji's opinion."

"Anthony!"

That oh-so-familiar timbre of voice roused him from his thoughts, he looked up and saw Benjamin Hunt busy making his way across the tables to join him. They exchanged a long embrace and a thread of emotion flashed across both their faces.

"I'm glad to see you again, Benji!" - then turned a flying glance in the direction of Dylan and David - "I hope you had a good trip."

"The blacker it is, the cleaner it is. What's that?" - Benji said in reply.

"Easy, the blackboard!" - Anthony replied smilingly.

"See David, that wasn't so hard!"

Anthony was growing more and more intrigued by the situation.

"Never mind Anthony." - Dylan interjected - "I had the worst trip of my life. Benji and David spent it challenging each other to riddles."

They burst into great laughter and attracted the curious glances of all those who were still present in the dining room at that hour. They had spent the trip very calmly, dealing with light topics and getting to know each other better as they had a tough journey ahead of them together. Before arriving at the hospital they had stretched out at the Concorde in Wallington, the hotel that Anthony had booked for Benji and which was less than four miles from the hospital. In no time Professor Hunt had done the check-in paperwork and left his trolley in the room, taking the opportunity for a rinse and a quick change of clothes. That cheerful atmosphere was the best way to start a long afternoon. During lunch, based on Scottish beef fillet accompanied by boiled potatoes and spicy sauces, Dylan and Anthony filled Benji in on the latest events, trying not to leave out any details. Professor Hunt, between bites, nodded with the expression of someone intent on grasping the smallest details.

"Very interesting." - he merely said from time to time.

David, who as usual seemed to be focused only on his plate, added with his mouth full - "Two absolutely normal girls, with normal lives and nothing really concrete that, as yet, suggests a connection between the two." They had come to the end of the story at lunch and there was a moment of silence where the three of them looked each other in the eye for any detail that had escaped their tale. Breaking the silence was Professor Hunt.

"Anthony, what can you tell me about sleep? How do the girls behave?" - Benji suddenly asked as he bit into a muffin.

Dr Green shuddered, turned to Dylan and said - "I told you, Benji is the one for us." It was then that he remembered to fill them in on what he had discovered that morning. He recounted how he was not initially surprised to find an accelerated heartbeat in the two patients and that all their attention, in the first few days, was exclusively focused on stabilising the rhythm to avoid aggravating an already complex clinical picture. Then that morning he casually glanced at Lisa Lawson's ECG trace and noticed something really strange. While, during the sleep phase, Sally Smith's heartbeat recovered an apparent normality only to accelerate again as soon as she woke up, Lisa's heartbeat was still accelerated.

"The physical body tends towards self-preservation, that is, it spontaneously tends to preserve, as far as it can, its integrity." - Benji intervened - "In Lisa's case, her mind might be in a state of continuous wakefulness and, probably, she is constantly living in a reality that she does not like and that leads her heart to maintain that state of excitement typical of those under stress, anxiety, or simply excited or terrified."

The three remained in strict silence as they waited for Professor Hunt to continue his examination.

"At the moment, it's not like I can tell you much else." - he continued - "For now, I am relying solely on your stories, but I have an idea that Dylan's hypothesis might have more of a basis."

"What do you want us to do?" - Anthony asked - "Your presence here is not yet official and therefore, within this hospital, we must move extremely carefully."

"Let me see one of the two girls." - she replied calmly.

He also asked for the availability of a room that was quiet and away from prying eyes - "In the room, only you may be present, at a distance and in strict silence. I don't want relatives, friends, nurses or anyone else to disturb us." - Benji stipulated. Dr. Green was well aware of what he was risking in making such a decision on his own, but he was aware that, up to that point, his efforts had not led to any improvement in the clinical picture of the two girls. He looked at Dylan and nodded.

"Good." - Dylan intervened - "I'll find a way to make Benji's presence official as soon as we get an initial feedback. I'll stay here with you." - Then he turned to his right - "You David are going to pop over to the Roman London Museum in St Helier and see if you can work a miracle."

"Right Dylan, it will be done." - David replied - "Although I won't deny that I would have loved to stay here with you."

"One last effort, David. I know it's a weak lead but we have to try them all without wasting any more time."

Something does not add up

It was now five o'clock in the afternoon. Dylan had taken advantage of a moment's break to call home and warn that he would most likely not be home in time for dinner.

"The fact that David is not coming tonight is great news since the pantry has been begging for mercy for two days." - joked Sara.

She knew her husband's job well. Her only worry was that something might happen to him but she had never complained about those times when he was absent from home or returned at the oddest times, even in the middle of the night.

"Each to his own." - she repeated to herself in such cases.

And his job was to take care of the house and the family, and he did it very well. In the early days she had worked as a cashier at a mini market on the London Road but, when Janet was born, they agreed that the best solution would be for her to look after the family exclusively. At first she wasn't entirely convinced that this was the right decision, but a couple of years later, the results of the ultrasound scan, which showed the twins on the way, were enough to dispel her doubts. Of course, the money wasn't a lot but, as they didn't have a mortgage or rent to pay, they lived more than decently on Dylan's salary, even though it was rare to be able to put anything aside at the end of the month. Dylan had just interrupted the conversation when he saw a nurse coming from down the corridor, pushing Sally's cot, followed like a shadow by Mr. and Mrs. Smith confabulating amongst themselves. A few steps away he could recognise the unmistakable gait of Dr Green. Anthony had insisted on starting with Sally Smith because, although she had been in hospital for much less time than Lisa, she was the one with the worst clinical condition. The girl continued to have both arms tied to the side of the bed, at the height of her elbows and wrists, with her hands rigidly bandaged. Although she continued to move her mouth, Sally no longer made any sound, no further calls for help, but there were more and more moments when she furiously tried to wriggle free of her arms. Benji made no objection as, for him, one patient was as good as another. Dr Green introduced Inspector Walker to Agatha and Wilford Smith, then they all entered a large room, number F389. Anthony had chosen that room not because it had any particular equipment but only because it was on the third floor and in an even less busy corridor, with most of the rooms empty or used as offices. In Building F, the first floor was reserved for doctors' offices, the second for patients' rooms and the third was the so-called emergency floor, where there were rooms that could be used in case of need and some offices used by authorised university researchers. On that Sunday there would be no one there to bother. Dylan looked around. Along the left side was a small two-seater sofa and three chairs with red plastic seats and steel legs. In front of the entrance, a wall about seven metres long was dominated by a large window under which a series of succulent plants were on display, all different but neatly arranged from left to right, from the smallest to the largest, with the latter not exceeding six inches in height. Instead on the right was a desk resting centrally on the wall with a comfortable black leatherette office chair, swivelling and with castors. Hanging on the wall above the desk was what, at first glance, appeared to be a reproduction of a composition on white by Kandinsky, while to the far right of the wall was a door with a clearly visible tag indicating the presence of an en suite bathroom. The nurse positioned the cot in the centre of the room, then stood waiting for instructions. Dr. Green had warned Mr. and Mrs. Smith that they would have to do some checks on Sally before they could proceed with her transfer there, to building F, the same building where Lisa Lawson was admitted. They would be very lengthy checks and he advised the Smiths to take advantage of the circumstance to finally take a break and spend some time with each other, knowing that their daughter would be in good hands.

"Take the gentlemen to the bar and tell Elaine to put everything on my bill." - He turned to the nurse as he waved the Smiths out of the room reassuring them - "Rest assured, I will call you as soon as I am done. Just a reminder that it may take a few hours to finish all the tests."

As Agatha and Wilford Smith disappeared down the corridor to the right, taking the first flight of stairs, out of a room on the left emerged Agent Thomas followed by what must have been Agent Harris.

"Agent Thomas, welcome. Punctual as a Swiss watch." - Dylan greeted him with a smile, then extended his hand towards his colleague.

"Constable John Harris, Inspector."

Those guys had had a rough time a couple of nights before but they'd proved their worth.

"First of all I must compliment you, you have performed admirably." - Dylan knew he owed Agent Thomas something - "As for Miss Smith's constant pleas for help, she should know that they were not directed at her. She couldn't have done it any other way. Great job."

Dylan noticed an expression of relief on her face. Then, turning again to both of them, he added - "What I can tell you for now is that we're going to try to figure it out in there. In order to do that, we must not be disturbed in any way, by anyone or for any reason. So the two of you will position yourselves out here and make sure to keep out anyone who tries to get in. It could take ten minutes or a few hours. I can't tell you more but I know I can trust you."

"Thank you Inspector." - Constable Thomas snapped to attention and positioned himself on the side of the door near the entrance handle while Constable Harris took his place a few feet away in the direction of the corridor access door.

Dylan entered the room and locked the door.

"You can come out now Benji." - Announced Anthony, who was standing by Sally's cot at that moment.

"Half a day's flight from the US to London to end up locked in a hospital bathroom for half an hour." - Professor Hunt exclaimed as he entered the room.

Dylan smiled, he was becoming convinced that David and Benji had been separated at birth. Then the eyes of the three turned to Sally Smith. Professor Hunt first asked Dylan to help him move the desk to the centre of the room, next to the cot, then turned to them both and invited them to take their seats at the far end of the room.

'I will show you, as I go, what to do. Now stay there, in silence.".

Dylan and Anthony both sat down on the sofa, taking care to put the ringers of their mobile phones on silent mode. Benji opened his black briefcase and pulled out a small table lamp, an extension cord and a universal travel adapter. He carefully placed it on the table and, once connected to the electrical socket, switched it on. He calmly walked to the large window and pulled down the blinds. The room was now lit exclusively by the lamp on the table and Dylan could make out the faint blue light it emitted. Using the handle on the bottom of the cot, Benji half lifted the backrest and looked Sally fixedly in the eyes. Then he pulled what appeared to be an old pocket watch out of its case and began swinging it about a foot away from the girl's face.

Right.

Left.

Right.

Left.

He whispered a few words that, from where they were sitting, Anthony and Dylan could hardly understand. He continued like that for at least twenty minutes. Every now and then he rested his hand on the girl's forehead, then suddenly his tone of voice began to be more assertive.

"Now you're calm and relaxed."

"Sally, now you can finally talk."

Benji kept swinging that sort of pendulum in front of her eyes. For Dylan, visibly tense, it was the first time he had witnessed a hypnotic session and, until then, he had thought that such scenes only existed in the movies.

"Sally, I now wish you to go back in your memory to your tenth birthday.".

Right.

Left.

Right.

Left.

"Who was with you that day celebrating?"

It was then that Sally, contrary to all predictions, began to speak and recount in a serene voice her day of celebration. Professor Hunt for the next half an hour pressed the girl, making her relive ever closer situations, until she reached the last period.

"No, it wasn't a good end-of-year party."

"And for what reason Sally?"

"Flu. I was sick and stayed home."

"Good girl Sally, now let's take another step forward. Cast your mind back to the first of February, the first day of this month. Tell me what you see?"

For the first time since they had started the session, the girl gasped and did not answer. Then Benji gently placed a hand on her forehead, whispered something as if to calm her down and resumed swinging the pendulum.

Right.

Left.

Right.

Left.

After a couple of minutes he tried again to ask - "Lisa, where were you on the first of February at noon?"

Lisa began to shake her head in rapid, short, discontinuous movements, then suddenly calmed down.

"On a plane. At noon I was on a flight to Cairo."

"That's good Sally, tell me briefly the highlights of that day, the ones you consider to be most important to you." - he gently invited her to continue - "Why were you on a flight to Cairo?"

"My parents had given me a weekend in Egypt."

Sally had obvious difficulties remembering and her narrative was no longer so fluid.

"Were you alone or with some friends?"

"Alone."

"Egypt is a beautiful place. Why did you want to go there?" - he pressed her.

"I had wanted to visit the Pyramids for a long time."

"Go on Sally, tell me about your trip."

"I had a stopover at Cairo International Airport in the late afternoon and took a taxi to the hotel."

"Do you remember the name of the hotel, Sally?"

A slight gasp accompanied a firm "No."

"That's okay Sally, go on, look at the hotel and tell me what you see."

Sally did not reply.

"Relax Sally, forget about the hotel. Tell me about dinner. What did you have good food on the night of the first of February?"

"Bangers and Mash."

Benji had no idea what it was but said - "Great, and where did you eat it, in a restaurant?".

"No, at home."

"At home?"

"Yes, at home."

"And who was at home with you?" - Benji asked uncertainly.

"I was with mum and dad."

Professor Hunt betrayed a bewildered expression for a moment but immediately composed himself and continued. - "Well Sally. After dinner what did you do?"

After a long pause Sally shook her head and said - "Nothing, I went to bed early because the next morning I had the excursion to the Pyramids planned."

"What's the last thing you remember before you fell asleep?"

"The kiss on my father's forehead."

"Good Sally, now relax and let's take a break. You stay here, calm and relaxed."

Professor Hunt stood up, careful not to make any noise, and walked towards Dylan and Anthony.

He wiped his forehead and wiped a cloth over his glasses.

He needed a break too, especially in that tangled situation.

"I don't know... everything was fine, but now there's something wrong." - he confided, taking care to keep his voice low - "Sally is perfectly in a trance and even her arms have stopped shaking. Yet these last memories are particularly hazy."

Anthony didn't know what to say but tried to speculate anyway. Dylan had been scratching his forehead for a couple of minutes, then he picked up his mobile phone and started typing something. It wasn't more than three minutes later that the display lit up.

SMS arrived from David.

'I confirm that Sally was at the Roman London Museum in St Helier on 2 February. I have also heard from Mrs Smith by phone who told me that her daughter has never been to Egypt. What on earth is going on?'

As soon as Benji read the message he had an epiphany - "A false memory induced." - He stood up - "Great shot Dylan, now we can move on. Let's see what Sally has to tell us that's interesting."

Claustrophobia

It could not have gone better. On arrival at Cairo International Airport, Sally was greeted by such grey skies that for a moment she thought she had never left London. Instead, when she woke up the next day, she had discovered that a pleasant, sunny day would be waiting for her, with a temperature that, in the hottest hours, could exceed 20°C.

"Perfect!" - thought Sally, already quite excited because she had dreamt of such a day more than once in her life.

The Giza plain was there waiting for her, a few steps west of Cairo, the last frontier before the endless Sahara desert. Everything was perfectly organised. Transfer leaving at nine o'clock, first stop at the Great Sphinx that guards the plain and then the inevitable visit to the pyramids where she had also included entry to the pyramid of Cheops. A quick breakfast at the hotel, a last jump to the room to get the bag, a quick check... water... torch... smartphone... OK, everything was there. The journey, in a nine-seater minivan, was short and comfortable and he was pleased with the choice he had made from the many companies offering tours of the Giza plain. As he got closer he could begin to make out more clearly the details of the Pyramids rising majestically into the sky. Of course the view of them from the alleys of Cairo had also excited her, but seeing them now, so close up, was a unique sight. The driver made a slight diversions to the first stop of the day, the Great Sphinx. After a good four years of restoration it had been reopened to the public back in 2014 and Sally already imagined herself walking between its legs and admiring from below the grandeur of that work carved into the rock and about 20 metres high. Before leaving, she had read all those tales about the presence of secret chambers and dark tunnels inside the Great Sphinx and was fascinated.

What could she say?

Her expectation was amply repaid and she could not help but be astonished and open-mouthed before such magnificence. Between one photo and another and a few inevitable selfies, she began to walk along the right side of the Sphinx, brushing the centuries-old rock with her fingertips. Their guide had seemed rather lax - "I will gladly repay a closed eye with a hefty tip." - she thought as she went on, trying to capture the smallest details to indelibly imprint those fantastic moments in her memory. The temperature was perfect but perhaps he would have done well to take a hat with him as the sun was beating down more than expected. She looked around, first to the right, then to the left, and realised that she was alone. Her seven fellow adventurers, five Italians and a French couple, had probably lingered to take pictures between the Sphinx's legs.

"Just as well." - she thought.

He slipped the bag off his shoulders, picked up the small bottle and, leaning back on the rock, took a couple of sips of water. He stared at his feet and felt all the excitement of being in contact with a piece of history flow through him. It was at that moment that his gaze was drawn to a small stone that was a few centimetres in front of his right foot. It had a very peculiar shape, about the size of an English muffin. It looked like a miniature pyramid, proportionally much lower as its height should not exceed half the length of one side, but the four triangular faces, although damaged, were clearly visible. As he was stuffing the water bottle back into the bag, he instinctively put his right foot on it and tried to move it by pressing the tip. She did not have time to realise what was happening when, suddenly, the stone gave way under her weight, slipping about three centimetres into the ground, and the rock behind her snapped open, leaving her suspended in mid-air for an instant. She fell backwards, beginning to roll heavily on what she realised was a narrow stone staircase until, after perhaps twenty or so steps, she realised she had reached the bottom. Still dazed and in pain from her fall, she opened her eyes and tried to figure out where she was. There was a lot of dust in the hot, almost unbreathable air. She coughed and tried in vain to get to her feet as, with a resounding headbutt, she realised that the tunnel she was in was little more than a metre high. With his aching head in his hands, he distinctly heard a sombre noise coming from above as more clouds of dust rose from the trembling walls of the tunnel and the staircase was filled with debris descending from above. She raised her eyes in the direction of the beam of light that began to grow thinner and thinner and, terrified, she stared at it until she found herself in absolute darkness. Her respiratory rate increased, which only made her breathing even more laboured, poisoned by continuous coughing fits. He managed to pull off his shirt to put it in front of his mouth to stop the dust.

He tried to keep calm - "Reason, reason!" - he repeated to himself in his head, while his eyes filled with tears and without realising that he was already shouting desperate pleas for help.

The heat was unbearable and his mouth was now dry, clogged and full of a bitter earthy taste. In desperation he groped his way up the steps, but his attempt failed after a few steps, in front of a wall of debris. He tied his shirt around his face and tried to dig with his bare hands but managed to advance no more than a couple of steps. He only had a moment's respite when under his fingers he felt something familiar. His bag. He pulled it to him with a tug, rummaged inside and began sobbing as he grasped the torch. He sat down with his back against a wall, switched it on and placed it on the floor. He took the small bottle of water, washed his eyes quickly first, then put it to his mouth. He spat out the first sip, trying to clear the dust from his mouth, then drank. He tried to calm himself and with the help of the torch he looked around. The tunnel, just over a metre high, was a little less than two metres wide and on the side opposite the staircase it seemed to continue level. Despondently she looked to her left.

There was no chance of reaching the surface through there, she would never be able to make her way through - "To my eye there must be six or seven metres of debris to dig out." - she thought - "Impossible even for them to hear me from the surface".

Then she looked to her right and found no alternative but to try to continue on that side. He put the bag on his shoulder and began to crawl forward. The further she went into the burrow, the more she realised that the floor, walls and ceiling were smoother and smoother and she was able to advance with greater ease. At the same time, however, she noticed that the tunnel did not proceed perfectly level but sloped slightly downwards. She advanced for about a minute when, from a distance, she had the feeling that the tunnel was dead-end. In front of her, about five or maybe six metres away, the torch faintly illuminated a stone wall. She continued forward and noticed instead that the tunnel presented a fork in the road.

"Now where do I go? Right or left?" - he repeated to himself and thought about it at least a hundred times before making a decision.

There was no reasonable choice to be made. The tunnel on the right seemed to slope towards the surface, but with a quick calculation, relying on his sense of direction, it seemed to go even further into the heart of the Great Sphinx. The tunnel on the left continued its descent slightly but ran in the direction of the legs and the chances of finding a way out on that side seemed better. The heat continued to be disarming and, as the floor was now smooth and free of debris, she also took off her shoes and trousers and placed them in the bag. She took another sip and decided.

Left.

With small pauses to rest his aching knees, he advanced for at least another three minutes until the tunnel bent ninety degrees to the right. He leaned out and illuminated a wall about two metres away that marked the end of the tunnel.

"It doesn't make sense." - she thought in despair - "Why should there be such a long tunnel with no exit?".

She decided to move forward until she reached the wall and began tapping it with her torch and listening to the sound it made. She moved from right to left analysing the two metres of stone in front of her and she could tell it was a single block.

"I'll have to go back and try..." - she did not have time to finish her reasoning that the block of stone she was standing on shifted under her weight with a loud sombre noise, slowly lowering a few centimetres. Sally, frightened, tried to move away and, turning to go back, saw to her horror that there was no way out. The burrow was no longer there. She began to breathe rapidly, her heart in her throat as she emitted that first terrifying scream, aware that she was now hopelessly stuck in that narrow two-by-two-metre compartment. She began to bang furiously against one of the walls using the torch but it broke and the room plunged into darkness.

"Help!" - she began to shout and, in the process, realised that she had completely lost her bearings.

In despair, she first tried to move the first wall she came across by forceful shoving, then she began to use her hands by scratching in the cracks between the stones. Sally had now lost her mind and continued to dig furiously, with the only result of injuring her fingers, which, although she could not see them, were already covered with a damp mixture of blood, sweat and soil. Several minutes passed, perhaps an hour or two. Locked in there, time seemed to stand still. Then, exhausted, she slumped to the floor and was left alone with her tears.

"Sally."

"Sally, can you hear me?"

Right.

Left.

Right.

(Whispers) Left.

"I'm here Sally, I got you."

"Easy Sally, I got you."

Sally slowly moved her head in the direction of that reassuring voice. She was surprised to see a faint beam of warm light that had come to keep her company and that serenely embraced her. Suddenly she no longer felt alone and even that terrible taste of earth and dust had disappeared.

"I am saved." - she thought as real tears poured down her cheeks - "I am saved!". The girl stopped wriggling on the cot, her face suddenly calmed down and the muscles in her arms relaxed again.

"Good Sally, welcome back!" - concluded Professor Hunt, who with a lightning gesture of his left hand stopped the oscillation of that strange pendulum.

Sally blinked and looked around frightened - "where am I? Who are you?" - were her first words.

"Hi Sally, I'm Professor Hunt but you can call me Benji." - Then turning to Anthony he said with his best smile - "What do you say Dr Green, shall we free your arms? Shall we let in some light?".

He and Dylan had been sitting motionless on the couch the whole time, as if petrified, and neither of them could comprehend what they had witnessed, right there, less than ten feet from their eyes.

They looked at each other for a moment, then quickly sprang to their feet. Dylan walked over to the large window and raised the shutter to let in some light, but realised it was already dark outside. He looked at his wristwatch, an Emporio Armani that Sara had given him the previous Christmas, it read twenty-one.

"Man, it's been four hours!" - he thought.

Anthony meanwhile had turned on the small spotlights at the sides of the room thinking that the bright neon light might bother the girl, then walked over to the cot and untied her arms. Sally was still confused but Benji's voice and his face, which despite obvious fatigue showed serenity and satisfaction, continued to inspire a deep confidence in her. She began to feel the first pains coming from her hands and, after lifting them, realised they were both bandaged.

"You will get all the answers you want in due course, Miss Smith." - Dr Green intervened, gently placing a hand on her shoulder - "I think you should now think only of resting. Your parents are anxiously awaiting you."

He then turned in Dylan's direction. He nodded his head in the direction of the door, then said - "Are you ready to deliver the good news?"

It was ten minutes past twenty-one when the door opened. Mr. and Mrs. Smith, who were visibly tired and had been waiting for over three hours as they sat in the hallway, saw Inspector Walker stop in the doorway.

Dylan looked at them with smiling eyes.

"Sally is waiting for you." - he said.

The Roman London Museum

The sun had not yet reached the horizon when Sergeant Carter arrived near the Roman London Museum. He stopped the car in the large car park on the opposite side of the road and walked briskly towards the museum, hoping to be able to talk to someone in charge as it was close to closing time. David noticed that he had a lot of difficulty concentrating on what he was supposed to be doing and admitted to himself that he would much rather have stayed at James Barry's Hospital. Physically he was there but his mind always went back to lunch with Professor Hunt - "I wonder what those three must be doing." - he thought as he walked through the front door of the museum.

He turned right in the direction of the ticket office. The London Roman Museum was a small museum where archaeological finds dating back to Roman times were displayed. As he could remember, this must have been the first time he had ever set foot in such a place. Behind the counter, busy tidying up some brochures, was a girl who certainly did not expect to see visitors coming in at that hour - 'Sorry sir, we are closing. The museum closes at 6pm and admission is until 5pm." - she said in a friendly tone - "If you want you can take one of these brochures where the opening days and times are highlighted."

David smiled at her and pulled his ID card out of his breast pocket - "Don't worry Miss." - he hastened to reassure the girl - "I would like to know if it is possible to meet a museum manager. I have a couple of questions to ask about a rather urgent matter. A matter of a few minutes."

The girl picked up the phone and made an internal call - "Hello Director Harvey, it's Kathy from the ticket office. I've got the officer here -"

"Sergeant David Carter from S.I.P." - David pleaded.

"Yes, Sgt David Campbell from S.I.P. who would like to meet with you to ask you a few questions." - He paused briefly - "Fine, thank you."

"Carter, damn it! Not Campbell., Carter!" - he thought resignedly, with girls he just couldn't get one right.

"Take a seat, the manager is waiting for you in his office on the first floor. Enter here and go through the first room. At the end, moved to the right, you will find a door with an entrance reserved for authorised personnel. Go up the stairs and down the corridor. The director's office is in the last room. Practically up here." - He sketched a smile and nodded with his index finger to indicate the ceiling.

David thanked and stepped through a heavy red curtain into the museum. In front of him opened a large room about fifty metres long and a little less than six metres wide. It was not very well lit and he thought it was a ruse to highlight the glass display cases, which, by contrast, were very bright. After all, he knew little or nothing about museums. As he walked past amphorae, vases, helmets and many swords, he noticed that there were three large rooms on the left. In the first two there were benches and two giant screens that were probably projecting the history of the museum or that of the artefacts on repeat; the third was closed to the public, with a large black curtain and a sign saying 'room under construction'. He spotted the door, climbed the stairs and followed the girl's instructions, walking down the long corridor until he reached the last door, which was half closed. She made to knock but the door opened abruptly - "Agent Campbell!" - the director, a distinguished gentleman in his sixties with white hair, abundant at the nape of his neck as the top of his skull reflected the neon light of the room, greeted her cordially - "I heard your footsteps in the corridor."

"Director Harvey." - He replied, holding out his hand - "Carter, this is Sergeant David Carter. I'll only take a few minutes of your time."

"Ah, excuse me. I must have misheard your name on the phone. I'm at your disposal, have a seat." - the warden pointed to one of the two chairs in front of his desk, which was positioned in front of a four-foot French window leading out onto the balcony.

David sat down and waited for the director to take his seat. Then he leaned towards him and held out his smartphone, asking him to look at the picture on the screen.

'Beautiful, isn't it? The half-bust of the Emperor Marcus Aurelius. A great shot, isn't it?" - he asked, starting to rock on the flexible back of his chair visibly pleased - "It's barely 2019 but I'd be willing to bet anything that it will be considered the greatest find of the century here in England."

David struggled to understand and tried to find a way not to betray his complete ignorance on the subject.

"How about you tell me more about this amazing find?" - he asked, pretending to look around to admire some small artefacts on the shelves, perhaps reproductions or perhaps not, but it would make no difference to him anyway.

"What needs to be said I already said at the press conference on 1 February, when we temporarily opened the wing dedicated to the Roman artefacts found at Beddington Park." - began Director Campbell - "I was convinced that that stone coffin of Roman origin, discovered in 1930, was the prelude to something greater."

He went on to recount how he decided, despite not being able to count on much money, to undertake a small excavation project at the park fully funded by his museum. The risk was amply repaid and, among the various finds unearthed, the highlight was the half-bust of Emperor Aurelius.

"You must have seen the wing being set up as you walked through the room," he said.

"Yes of course, but what do you mean by temporary opening?" - David asked.

"Come and see, there are still posters outside in the car park. It's hard for you not to have seen them!" - she motioned him to get up and look out the window in the direction of the large car park.

It was past eighteen, the sun had disappeared over the horizon and the area was semi-deserted, apart from David's car there were only four others. What immediately attracted his attention were the large billboards, now well lit by the street lamps, which he had not really noticed when he arrived. He counted fifteen of them, six metres by three metres, positioned well apart, five on each side, around the perimeter of the car park. Apart from three billboards that reminded how that car park had, long ago, been home to a travelling circus, the Irish Circus of Mystery, the other twelve were all dedicated to the temporary opening, from 1 to 3 February 2019, of the Beddington Park finds wing.

"Concentrate David, concentrate!" - he thought to himself as he remembered how he had allowed himself to be too distracted by the afternoon's events.

He had not seen those billboards at all.

"I admit it was a well-thought-out marketing operation. A grand opening with pomp and circumstance, a press conference, and then an additional month of waiting to finish some set-up work that wouldn't have taken more than a couple of days anyway. We hope in this way to create a wait that will lead to an increase in visitors." - concluded the director - "We have some money to make up.".

David nodded and returned to his seat - "Do you have video surveillance in the museum?"

"Of course, all areas are covered."

"What if I told you that I would need the recordings of the days of 2 and 3 February?"

"I would tell you that we don't have anything older than a fortnight and therefore the first ones available would be those of..." - a quick glance at the desk calendar - "...by eye of 10 February. Sorry."

At that moment David's smartphone, which was still resting on the desk, vibrated. It was a text message from Dylan.

He frowned - "What the heck do the pyramids of Egypt have to do with it now?" - he thought.

Certain that he had nothing more to ask, he said goodbye to the manager, thanking him for his helpfulness, and prepared to retrace his steps towards the exit. In the meantime he carefully reread the message and called Mrs Smith so that he could answer Dylan's strange request. Arriving at the car park he looked again at the large billboards and thought again about how he could have missed them earlier.

"Yeah, maybe we could use a good magic sphere." - he thought as he looked at that big, pointy-hatted magician bent over the crystal ball in one of the circus billboards.

He got into his car and decided to first go to the station to pick up his Jeep and then head back to James Barry's Hospital. But not before grabbing a quick bite to eat in some café.

Victory!

It was just after twenty-thirty when David arrived on the third floor and ran into Officer Harris.

"I've been walking around the hospital for at least half an hour." - he exclaimed, nodding to the officer and sitting down in one of the chairs at the beginning of the corridor.

He had noticed out of the corner of his eye Mr and Mrs Smith at the end of the corridor next to Agent Thomas.

"Would you be so kind as to tell me what's going on?" - he asked in a whisper.

Constable Thomas made him aware of how Inspector Dylan had given orders not to let anyone into the room where Dr Green and Sally Smith were present besides him.

"Are you sure no one else is with them?" - he asked curiously.

"Without a shadow of a doubt, Sergeant."

"Strange." - he closed in a low voice, then leaned back and squinted his eyes.

At least another thirty minutes passed when the door to room F389 finally opened. From that distance he could not make out what Dylan was saying but he saw Mrs Smith put her hands over her face and run into the room followed by her husband. Dylan turned to him and made a victory sign. David and Agent Harris hurried forward because in a flash they had all poured into the room. Sally's parents were on either side of the cot and, with tears in their eyes, they were just stroking her face and whispering sweet words to her. Dylan and Anthony had stood a little apart and were confabulating with the visibly excited Agent Thomas. Not far from the cot was Benji who, with Olympian calm, was rearranging his briefcase.

"No one else was in the room, huh?" - smiled David, glancing sidelong at Officer Harris who was surprised by the presence of the man he had never seen before.

"I don't know why but I think this miracle is thanks to you. Wilford Smith and this is my wife Agatha." - Said Sally's father turning towards Benji who immediately looked in the direction of Dylan and Anthony to see what he should reply.

"Mr and Mrs Smith, officers." - Dylan promptly intervened - "We all owe Professor Hunt a thank you for what took place this evening but, for the moment, we cannot tell you any more than that and we also need to ask you for one more favour."

Everyone listened in silence as Wilford Smith continued to hold Benji's hand tightly. The next morning, no later than eight o'clock, they would try what Dylan called 'the new therapy' on Lisa Lawson, with the hope of getting the same good results. Dylan therefore asked everyone not to report anything that had happened, at least until the press conference that Chief Inspector Cooper would certainly hold the next afternoon. Dr. Green also assured Mr. and Mrs. Smith that he would arrange for a new room to be allocated for Sally's stay, right on that floor, away from prying eyes, and that she would be cared for by his trusted and highly qualified staff. No one presented any objections and everyone pledged to maintain the strictest silence. Dylan, after dismissing the officers and asking them to return the next morning, approached David and took him aside, briefly briefing him on what had happened.

'I have unfortunately not made any progress other than to confirm the presence of the two girls on the first weekend of the month at the Roman London Museum. Although it is not possible to establish the exact day, we are certain that they were there between the first and the third of February."

"Video cameras, recordings of those days, do we have anything?" - Dylan pressed him.

"Nothing, the recordings relating to that weekend have been overwritten. In addition, I stopped by the station and they confirmed that in the area where the girls were found, no recordings are useful for the investigation as the only two private surveillance cameras do not frame beyond the pavement." - David explained - "I also took the opportunity to thoroughly check the personal items found in Sally Smith's bag but found nothing new and arranged for everything to be returned to the family."

"Damn it!" - huffed Dylan, then with a consoling pat on David's shoulder he added - "It's OK, you were a great help to this girl anyway."

In the meantime, two nurses had arrived to take Sally to her new room, followed on sight by Mr and Mrs Smith, who thanked everyone for the umpteenth time before walking through the door. Now they were alone again. Professor Hunt, for the first time, showed his tiredness by sitting heavily on the sofa.

"Benji, how are you doing?"

"Very well but I have to admit it's been rather tough." - He took a pause to reflect.

Since he had finished the session he had been silent, apparently intent on tidying up his material.

"Already from the first few minutes I realised I was in front of a girl in an unusual psycho-physiological state, an uncommon trance state and one I had never encountered in the past, neither during my sessions nor, as far as I remember, I think I had ever read about it." - he picked up his glasses and began to clean the lenses with a small piece of cloth - "Initially it was difficult to make my way into his memories but, after all, am I or am I not the best?" - he then turned, smiling in Anthony's direction.

"Who's on the other side of the court? Who are we playing with?" - intervened Dylan.

Benji put on his glasses - "We are up against someone very good indeed. I don't deny that, even if I wanted to, I myself would not be able to achieve such results. Whoever he is, he uses some peculiar technique unknown to me to create what seemed to me to be a kind of virtual world that, for his victims, runs parallel to real life. ". He took another moment to collect his thoughts.

"I think he's still refining his methodology as we've all been able to notice small flaws in Sally's memories but, without a shadow of a doubt, we're up against someone who has an uncommonly good background in this field."

Dylan then turned to Anthony - "Thank you. Without your help I would still be groping in the dark."

"Well, in the end you had the right intuition Dylan. I just decided to go with the flow."

"Shall we play the long game? I say we can split the credit four ways and go rest. What do you say?" - David intervened in his usual manner.

They looked each other in the eye, all visibly tired but definitely satisfied.

"Yes David, you're right. Let's go rest." - Benji closed.

Old Man Hunt

That night, still full of adrenalin, after a couple of sandwiches grabbed on the fly at the hospital bar, everyone spent it as they saw fit. They returned to their homes, or hotels as in the case of Professor Hunt, with just under an hour to midnight. David drained a couple of cans of beer he had bought in the afternoon, on his way back from the museum, and chose to spend a couple of hours relaxing in front of his fifty-five-inch opting for an old Sergio Leone western film. But half an hour after it had started, he was already snoring on the sofa. Anthony immediately went to bed, still unsure how to assess the afternoon's events from a medical point of view, while Benji, before closing his eyes, spent a good hour online searching for any article that might be useful in this strange situation.

Dylan found Sara still awake waiting for him in his bedroom - "Phew... I'd almost given up hope!" - He uncovered the sheets and, in the soft light of a bedside lamp, revealed himself in a sexy hazel-coloured dressing gown.

Another hour passed before he fell sound asleep, visibly satisfied with how the day had ended. The next morning, at seven thirty, they were all gathered around a small table in the cafeteria of building F. Not far from them, seated at another table, were both the Lawsons, Robert and Clare, who had been urged the previous evening to both be present at the hospital that morning. Lisa had already been moved to the same room, on the third floor, where they had managed to revive Sally Smith, who had spent a fairly quiet night although she had, for the first time, shown the need to resort to painkillers to relieve the pain in her upper extremities. Dr Green had mentioned to the Lawsons the possibility that they would try an experimental therapy with Lisa that morning and, to reassure them, told them that they had had good results with Miss Smith.

"Hoping that everything will go well with Lisa as well, I have pre-alerted Chief Inspector Cooper." - Dylan recounted as they all sat down over a steaming cup of long coffee - "I got him out of bed at six-thirty and told him that, in all likelihood, he would have to set up a press conference for the afternoon. I didn't go into detail, but I did mention that he would also have to come up with a plausible excuse so that he could explain to the press how we had managed to solve the case."

"But we know very well that even if everything goes well with Lisa, we haven't solved a damn thing." - David intervened.

"You're right but we have to stall. We can't continue to keep out the press, which has behaved far too well so far. We have to make statements, but without too many details, at least until we have a clear picture."

"We will also make your presence official this afternoon." - He added, turning towards Professor Hunt - "And we will see to it that you issue a written request for cooperation that may be useful to justify your absence from the university."

Benji nodded. He knew well that they would not let him leave until the case was solved. At eight o'clock sharp, Agents Thomas and Harris also turned up. The only change from the previous evening was that Professor Hunt did not have to hide from the sight of the girl's parents, but was introduced by Dr. Green as one of his trusted associates before he locked himself inside the room. Lisa had now been in that state for over nine days and Mr and Mrs Lawson were now at the end of their tether. Visibly tired but finally with the bit of hope they had lost for too long, Robert and Clare sat silently down the corridor.

"All the same as yesterday." - Dylan exchanged a nod of understanding with the officers outside the door, then entered and closed it behind him.

Lisa Lawson sat on her cot, a blank stare turned towards the Kandinsky hanging in the centre of the room's right-hand wall. Her skin was even lighter than the last time Dylan had seen her. Her visibly reddened eyes stood out even more against her white face and, juxtaposed with her reddish hair, certainly did not give her a very reassuring appearance. Her skinny arms showed the first signs of malnutrition despite the fact that she was on parenteral artificial nutrition by intravenous injection. Unfortunately, it had not been easy, due to her particular clinical condition, to find an ideal protocol for her condition. Nevertheless, that morning, Dr. Green had ordered the nurses to temporarily remove the catheter in her vein with the excuse that they would have to move it to the other arm at the end of that therapy session anyway.

"Take a seat on the couch David and turn off the ringer on the phone." - Dylan recommended himself as he walked over to the window to close the blinds.

Anthony had temporarily switched on the spotlights and Benji maniacally repeated the same preparatory ritual as the night before. He put the back of the cot in the right position but Lisa had no desire to lie down.

"We only manage to get her to lie down when she seems to be falling asleep." - Anthony intervened - "Those are the only moments when she closes her eyes even though, as I mentioned to you yesterday morning, her heartbeat shows that she is not really resting."

"Then I will need your help. Position yourself behind him." - Professor Hunt established as he switched on the lamp - "Dylan, turn off the light."

A surreal silence descended again in the room as Benji began to swing the pendulum in front of Lisa's face. Finally Anthony, from that distance, was able to recognise it. It was an old pocket watch, made of bronze, which, if he remembered correctly, his friend must have received as a gift from his paternal grandfather. A long time ago, before his death, he had also presented it to him. On their way back from a Red Sox game they had dropped by his house because Benji had to retrieve some books that they would both need to complete a research project. Old Hunt was a man of great learning and Benji owed to him his passion for the study of the human mind, what, that day, his grandfather called the most valuable safe in the world.

"Whoever manages to open it will become the richest man in the world," - he told him as if to justify himself, but then he did not pause to explain that, for him, the rich man was not the one who possessed the most money but the one who would enjoy true knowledge.

He still remembered how astonished he was when he entered that half-dark room, which was somewhere between an ancient library and a magic laboratory. The two side walls were completely occupied by shelves overflowing with dusty books that reached up to the ceiling while, in the centre of the room, there was an old desk, overflowing with papers, ampoules and strange drawings, sketched in pencil, on large white sheets of paper thrown about in confusion. On the opposite wall stood a large black board full of formulas and geometric figures trying to stand out within a white cloud, a clear sign of recent erasure. On the floor was so much chalk dust that the room probably hadn't seen a hoover in at least a decade. Below the blackboard was a second desk with a sort of wall formed by old books piled up on its front edge, hiding old Hunt, hunched over his papers, illuminated by a lamp that diffused a faint blue light into the room. Now that he thought about it, the lamp

Benji was now using must have been just that, or at least looked a lot like it.

"Don't stare at the pendulum." - Benji admonished him, sketching a smile and bringing him back to reality - "There, now you can help me stretch it out."

Unable to tell how much time had passed, Anthony shook his head, squinted his eyes and gently laid Lisa down on the cot. He took her pulse and began to count in his head. He noted that her heartbeat was slowing, then nodded in his friend's direction and walked away, still a little dazed, joining David on the couch. Dylan had chosen to sit on one of the red chairs this time and watched attentively with his torso leaning forward. Benji started in the same way, resuming swinging the pendulum at irregular intervals and whispering a few words to the girl. Then he started to ask her some questions, the same ones he had used with Sally but this time he did not get any results. Initially, Lisa did not seem to want to answer any questions, which caused Professor Hunt, who already had sweat on his forehead, serious difficulties. A good half hour passed, then he finally found the right key to break through - "Lisa, can you tell me the last day you remember anything?"

"25 May 2003." - she replied in a hushed voice.

"The 25th of May 2003? It's been a long time since then."

"Yes, I've been waiting for many days."

Autophobia

That day she would become a young lady. Dad Robert had been repeating that phrase to her like a mantra for at least a week. Lisa, like every morning, had woken up in her parents' bed clinging to Mum Clare. That day, too, her father Robert decided that he would try to convince the little one to start sleeping in her bed - "You're a big girl now, young lady, from tonight you'll have your own bed!"

"Come on Robert, at least today is her birthday!" - Clare intervened - "Don't listen to your father Lisa, he's joking. You can sleep with mum as often as you like."

The father had never approved of that situation and, although he had never confided in his wife, he was beginning to be very worried by his daughter's morbid attitudes. But that morning he quickly realised he had to let it go and looked out of the window of their beautiful hotel room overlooking the sea. It had been Mum Clare's idea to give little Lisa a week's holiday in the Maldives for her sixth birthday and that would be the last day on the beautiful Gan Island. The weather forecast was the same as it had been for the previous days, with good weather, heat, lots of humidity and occasional showers. They had chosen to spend that holiday in the southern atolls because that period is certainly not the best time to spend in the Maldives. In fact, while in the atolls to the north the monsoon would bring a lot of rain towards the end of the month, in the south the weather would gradually improve with sunny days and increasingly rare rainfall. Even that day seemed no different from the others with clear skies and the usual clouds on the horizon, the same clouds that had only twice in the previous six days managed to reach their island. At the end of the day they considered themselves very lucky because, having encountered good weather, they had managed to enjoy that holiday wonderfully in complete relaxation since there were not many tourists present and many rooms in their hotel were actually empty. They had also managed to spend a couple of days in complete serenity on a small beach that they had found not far from the hotel and which no one frequented. The holidaymakers preferred to stay on the large white beach, which was just a stone's throw from the hotel and offered all kinds of services, from umbrellas to sunbeds, from Wi-Fi to a well-stocked bar that was always open. That last morning Lisa asked to spend it on the elephant beach, as she had nicknamed it because in the centre of the small bay there was a large rock emerging from the water and which, according to the child's imagination, looked just like a large elephant. The thing that had pleasantly surprised Robert throughout the holiday was that little Lisa had shown greater autonomy and he had not infrequently found himself calling her back when, intrigued by the wonders around her, she tended to wander off to the beach in search of shells or to follow some colourful fish in the water. Normally Lisa would never stray further than their shadow, especially when she was in new places.

"Maybe Clare got it right this time." - she thought whenever she saw her daughter take some distance from them, forgetting her fears.

So that morning, after a sumptuous breakfast buffet, they headed for their secret little beach. It took about twenty minutes to reach it. The small bay was now within reach of their eyes when Lisa, under her wide-brimmed straw hat, broke the silence - "I forgot my floaties on the breakfast table." Lisa couldn't swim and would never have entered the water without her trusty floaties. Her father immediately offered to go back and retrieve them. After all, this was her birthday and everything had to be perfect! Robert retraced his steps while little Lisa and her mother continued towards the beach. He looked up at the sky again and saw that the grey clouds on the horizon had moved a little closer and noticed that a light breeze was picking up. He decided that he would lengthen his pace so that he would be back in less than half an hour. Meanwhile on the elephant beach the usual ritual was taking place. Clare first spread out the two towels under the shade of a beautiful palm tree, which had grown at an unusual angle to the ground, then she took Lisa's hat off and began to rub sunscreen all over her body. He then took the small inflatable pool from his duffel bag. No higher than 30 centimetres and with a diameter of about one metre, it had been the best purchase made on the spot since Lisa spent most of her days inside it.

"I'm going to surprise Robert." - she thought as she moved her mouth closer to the safety valve, starting to pump her breath as fast as she could.

"Good mum, you're doing it again!" - said Lisa happily.

She did not think it could be so tiring, but in the end, satisfied, she handed the small pool to Lisa.

"By now Robert will be on his way back." - she thought as she looked at her watch.

It had taken her a good ten minutes to inflate it but she was proud of the result. Tired she lay down and resumed reading 'Iceberg', one of the few Clive Cussler books she had not yet read. That blessed pool had made her sweat and she thanked the breeze for bringing her some relief. Lisa took the pool and dragged it with her until she reached the shore. That morning the sea was not as calm as the previous day's, but those small waves, still superficial, were not enough to stir the sand and the water, still perfectly clear, did not hide the seabed.

She entered the water and began to peer through the sand in search of some small fish - "Today I'm sure at least one of them will end up in my bucket... but where is it?" - she wondered as she looked around.

She remembered that she had forgotten it at the hotel and thought - "Ah well, Dad will certainly notice and bring it to me along with the floaties.".

A gasp. Suddenly he realised that he was standing with his feet in the water and without his armrests. He had an unexpected panic attack. He immediately felt his breathing quicken and his back was racked with strange cold shivers. She wanted to call her mother with all her might but was as if petrified. The only handhold that seemed to give her some comfort was the small pool that she realised she was clutching with all her strength.

She did not think twice about it and jumped on board the small pool, which immediately buckled under her weight and filled with water. She began to tremble, her teeth clenched and her hands clenched tightly on the edge. She tried to keep still because every little movement risked her toppling over into the water. Not a word could come out of her mouth. The water was no higher than a foot and she wanted to scream, throw herself into the water and run to safety in her mother's arms. Instead she stood there, motionless, staring wide-eyed at the receding shore. Lulled by the waves and buoyed by the cool breeze, the small pool began to head out to sea. For Lisa, time stopped at that precise instant. She could not even remember how much had passed. She could still make out the palm trees in the bay, the large rock sticking out of the water, further to the right what looked like a structure, perhaps the hotel, and then that coloured dot that must have been her mother still intent on reading her book.

"Yet she's always there... I see her... she's so small... Mum help me... I'm here... why don't you come?"

"You're not alone Lisa. I found you."

Lisa Lawson, on her hospital bed, began to show signs of waking up.

"Let's go back to shore, Lisa. Do you want to come with me?"

"Yes." - she replied, as her face suddenly seemed to brighten.

"Good. Now close your eyes and sleep. When you wake up you will be in your mother's arms." - And finally Lisa Lawson closed her eyes and fell into a deep sleep.

"OK guys, that's gone too." - Benji said with great satisfaction, turning in the direction of the three who continued to watch him in amazement - "How about you guys do something too?"

While Anthony was busy raising the shutter, Dylan looked at his watch. This time, despite the initial difficulties, the session had lasted less than the previous one, almost three hours, and Lisa was among them again.

"What a sight! And without even having to pay for a ticket." - David had nestled himself into the sofa, one leg crossed, arms along his sides and an expression that showed enormous satisfaction - "Pity about the absence of popcorn but at the cinema it would have been at least ten minutes of applause."

Benji smiled and gave a hint of a bow. They then all gathered around the cot together.

"Well done Benji." - Anthony put his arm around him - "Very impressive."

It was then Dylan's turn who limited his compliments to a nod and then asked - "What can you tell me again Benji? Do you think this is the work of the same person?" Professor Hunt took a seat in the chair and with a swift gesture of his foot he pushed himself backwards, making the wheels travel about two metres. Then he began to turn around until he stopped - "I would say yes, one individual, very good and able to master several techniques. I could see two big differences from Sally Smith."

"Anything that might be useful for the investigation." - Dylan urged him.

"Sally Smith was imprisoned in a place she did not know. I don't understand what technique was used to place her in that sort of virtual reality but the result was truly remarkable. Moreover, Sally had an experience that led her to experience one of the worst nightmares the human mind can imagine. The feeling of being stuck in an underground chamber, with no way out, is similar to that of being buried alive. Claustrophobia and taphophobia have points in common, and although few people actually suffer from it, anyone can be terrified by the mere thought of it."

He took off his glasses and began wiping them off with a small piece of cloth, which he pulled out of his right pocket - "On Lisa, I think it went more smoothly. I didn't notice any smears in the girl's story. I could almost bet that Lisa really was on that island. Moreover, this time our friend has exploited a weakness already present in this girl's mind." He then turned in Dr Green's direction - "Anthony, may I advise you to combine medical therapy with a consultation with an excellent psychologist." - A further pause - "For her and also for her mother."

"Yeah." - David intervened - "Maybe more for the mother."

"I don't know if this information will be of any use to you, but that's the best I can tell you." - Benji got up from his chair and began to put everything back into the briefcase - "I'd say we can give Mr and Mrs Smith the good news."

Heading for the door Dylan picked up his smartphone and glanced at the display - "Eighteen unanswered calls."

He immediately turned to David.

He too had just picked up his phone and returned the same look - "Oh, fuck!"

Alan Baker

"I've been trying unsuccessfully for two hours to reach you, where the heck have you been?" - On the other end of the phone was Chief Inspector Martin Cooper, shouting out any kind of profanity he could think of. On the third floor of James Barry's Hospital, more precisely in room 9 in corridor 8, a situation bordering on the tragicomic was taking place. Anyone who had arrived there at that moment would have witnessed a scene that was surreal to say the least. On one side of the room was Sergeant David talking animatedly with Constable Thomas, in the centre were Mr and Mrs Smith visibly moved confabulating by Lisa's bed with a smiling Dr Green, a little further away was Benji who had resumed arranging his briefcase with his usual calmness and, in the doorway, Dylan trying to reason with the chief over the phone.

"Got it boss. Yes, boss. Good. All clear. Let's pop over to the ER and then I'll catch up with you as soon as I can." - In the meantime he called David back, motioning for him to follow - "Try to keep the press at bay a little longer by calling a conference later this afternoon."

They began to descend the stairs to reach the first aid station - "Yes boss, I have some important news, I'll update you in the office. See you in a bit." - He ended the call by turning to David - "So what's the news?"

"Officer Thomas told me that about two hours ago they took a guy to hospital who suddenly started freaking out, right here in Beddington Park. He knew immediately that the station was looking for us but decided not to disturb us by following orders. He still decided to send Constable Harris to take a look anyway." - David was already breathing heavily - "Unfortunately, from what he told him over the phone, it seems that the huddle of reporters outside the entrance to the emergency room reformed as soon as word got out about the boy's strange behaviour. That's all he could tell me."

Dylan flipped through the phonebook and initiated a call - "Hello Anthony? It's Dylan. Try to get the Lawsons sorted out as soon as possible, join us in the ER and warn Benji that he'll probably have to work overtime this morning."

"Skipping lunch again today, huh?"

"David, does that sound like time?"

It took them a couple of minutes to reach the emergency room, passing through the inner corridors to avoid the reporters. At the red door stood three officers, Constable Harris and probably the two from the Met who had intervened in the park.

"Inspector Dylan Walker of S.I.P." - He hastened to introduce himself.

"Hello Inspector. We had orders to stake out the area until you arrived... well, over two hours ago..." - he paused to emphasise the lateness with which he had introduced himself - "The case is yours. We have reported everything there is to know to Agent Harris." - Finished one of the two officers.

"Ah, good luck." - he added after turning on his heel.

The two agents walked away talking to each other and one of them couldn't hold back a giggle.

"We're in danger of becoming the laughing stock of the police force here if we don't get a move on and sort this out." - David pointed out annoyed.

"Don't worry David, I already know how to patch it up today. Now let's see what they have to say here." - He knocked and opened the door.

There was probably a time when they would have been amazed to witness such a scene but this time they didn't bat an eyelid when they saw the guy in his thirties struggling furiously on the stretcher, imprisoned in what appeared to be some kind of straitjacket.

"They found him inside the park, along one of the paths that runs alongside the River Wandle. Officers were alerted by witnesses who reported how the initially calm boy suddenly started running around, flailing like a madman from side to side or rolling on the ground, tearing his clothes, screaming for them to leave him alone. They were helped by at least four nurses to manage to stop him." - Agent Harris briefed them.

It was at that moment that behind the three the door opened again and Dr. Green entered.

"I understand." - was all he said in Dylan's direction as he walked towards a doctor who was trying to manage the complicated situation with three other nurses.

They talked for a few minutes, then the doctor ordered one of the nurses to accompany the boy, following Dr Green's directions, and two others to find the clearest path so that no one would see him. Two nurses came out first, together with Agent Harris, then in order Anthony, Dylan, David and immediately behind the stretcher pushed by the nurse.

"Alan Baker, 31 years old from Watford. They spotted him through the paperwork. The family have already been notified and he is en route. The only thing we know is that even they can't explain why their son is here in London." - Anthony immediately made them aware of what the emergency room doctor had told him.

Although he was well known and respected, it had not been easy to convince that doctor to hand over the patient to him - "In two days I have broken as many protocols as I have ever done in my entire career." - he thought to himself. They reached room F389 again, with Agent Thomas still standing near the entrance, and while the two nurses stood along the corridor with Agent Harris, the third entered pushing the gurney. He found himself in the semi-darkened room, lit only by a faint blue light with a man he didn't know in the middle, sitting on a swivel chair and smiling as he swung his head. Benji was actually anything but happy but the unfortunate nurse just couldn't know it.

"Everything OK here?" - He asked turning towards Dr Green - "You say I can go?"

"Yeah sure, everything's fine. We'll take it from here." - Interjected David immediately zapped with a look from Anthony.

That 'we'll take it from here' didn't entirely reassure him but the nurse turned and walked out of the room.

"Mah... what did I say wrong?" - whispered David as he made his way back to the couch.

Dylan meanwhile, in addition to the usual recommendations, had warned Agent Thomas to contact him by text message if he had any news.

This time, he would keep his smartphone in sight. Then he called Chief Inspector Cooper and advised him to call the press conference for eighteen o'clock directly there, at James Barry's Hospital, building F, third floor.

He would not be able to get through to the office.

Tomophobia

It was more than ten hours until the start of the game. They had never emerged victorious from Stamford Bridge but Alan was more than certain that this time his Watford would return home from that stadium with the three points in their pockets.

"Well, I've still got some time to sober up from last night." - He thought to himself as he walked into Beddington Park taking a quick glance at the clock.

Nine forty-five. He had slept little and badly that night. He had reached London the previous evening and, together with two friends, for a handful of pounds had found accommodation at a hostel in Beddington near Brandon Hill Cemetery. At that price he didn't expect much but he certainly didn't expect to find himself on a mattress that, he could bet, had been in use for over thirty years. He still couldn't understand how Tim and Andrew could sleep so soundly. Instead he, despite the night's revelry, was already up at eight o'clock, his back in pieces. He had tried in vain to wake them up, then decided to give up and thought it would be healthy to take a walk around the area. He had started walking, following the signs indicating Beddington Park and, after a good stretch on Croydon Road, although he felt tired, he decided to take a closer look when he reached the entrance. As it was still early and knowing that they would not leave the hostel until fourteen o'clock, he calculated that he still had a good couple of hours to visit the park.

"I'll reach the River Wandle, lie down under a tree for an hour or so and then head back." - he calculated at the sight of a sign along the footpath indicating a distance of thirty minutes to reach that river.

On the way, he was not surprised to notice that there were many people who had decided to take advantage of that beautiful day.

The temperature was ideal and there were those who took their dogs on leashes, those who did gymnastics or those who took advantage of the large areas of green grass simply to kick a ball around. He was satisfied with his decision, he had done the right thing in getting up from that stupid bed. He walked briskly but, after not even five minutes, he began to feel the effects of that sleepless night. He had really walked a lot.

"Remember Alan, you also have to go back." - He took a right and decided to leave the marked path, heading in a straight line towards an area rich in vegetation and which must surely be close to the river.

He estimated that, with that diversions, he would reach the River Wandle saving at least ten minutes. When he reached the river bank he could only be fully satisfied with the result. In fact, by the looks of it, he had saved even more than ten minutes but, on the other hand, he had walked through tall grass and his canvas tennis shoes were now completely wet. He looked around and saw, about a hundred metres to his left, a small levelled area, close to an old brick bridge. Beyond the bridge there was clearly another path and he thought that he would probably have to return by following the signs on the other side of the river.

He did not dare to think about how much time he would lose but decided that at that moment the priority was to take off his shoes and try to dry them by leaving them for at least an hour in the sun. As he reached the bridge he noticed that the area was not that busy, since until then he had only seen, far from him, an old man who was now already fading from his sight. Under an old beech tree he saw a wooden bench. He looked around and thought that this was the perfect place to rest for a while. He took off his shoes and socks and put them in the sun, placing them on top of a pile of broken bricks that were on the ground to the right of the bridge. Then he sat down. The bench, no more than five feet long, had the top plank of the backrest broken and so what was left came right down the middle of his back - "Even the bench is uncomfortable. Not one of them fits." - he muttered. He tried to change position, lying on his back with his legs bent and his bare feet on the ground. A light breeze caressed his face as the gentle sound of the river's waters began to lull his thoughts and gently accompanied him into the arms of Morpheus. Time passed quickly while Alan was busy chasing his dreams, deeply asleep on that old bench in Beddington Park. He was suddenly awoken by a cold shiver that ran down his backside to his shoulders.

He jumped up and realised he was all achy - "Damn bench!" - he said, gnashing his teeth.

He blinked, still groggy from sleep. It had grown dark.

"Nineteen fifty." - he noted after a quick glance at his watch - "I slept almost nine hours! Shit, the game!" - he picked up his smartphone and noticed that it still had the ringer off from the night before.

Thirty-seven unanswered calls, the box indicating incoming messages lit up and - "Oh, no!" - the battery at 1%.

He was not in time to unlock the keyboard that, with a slight vibration, the smartphone switched off.

"Fuck the game!" - he shouted, starting to look around.

He realised that, despite everything, it was not so dark. The moonlight combined with the distant lights of the city meant that he could see, at least as far as he was interested.

He retrieved his socks and shoes - "At least these are dry." - and sat back down on the bench, lifting his right foot to put on the first sock.

He noticed a distant light he hadn't seen before, very bright - "It must be a street lamp, I'll head in that direction. I should still find someone around the park at this time." - he said aloud as if he had someone to talk to.

He placed his foot on the ground and lifted his left. As he put on the second sock he looked up again. He stopped and squinted. Something did not convince him.

That light.

That light had not been so close before.

In fact, now it seemed even stronger and higher than the horizon.

He speculated at first that it might be a torch being used by someone running in the dark in the park, but now it was going too fast, with quick jerks from right to left. It was getting closer.

Faster and faster.

Too fast.

A sudden flash dazzled him before he could even get up from the bench. He was flooded with mixed emotions, fear and relief, too scared to try to move, he felt light at the same time, as if he were floating on air. Then, suddenly, just so much light, silence and the switch went off. He could not know how much time had passed, nor did he have time to turn his thoughts to it. He awoke to a stabbing pain invading his head. He tried to scream but the pain was compounded by more pain. No sound came out of his mouth and his lips, held in place by what looked like staples, began to bleed.

He could see himself clearly.

He was lying on a strange white cot, his arms and legs spread, his wrists bound and his ankles locked. Alan could see a metal ring that, positioned at the level of his neck, prevented him from lifting his head. He could not move it, neither to the right nor to the left, but was forced to look fixedly above him, where there was a large mirror and many small LEDs on the sides that illuminated him brightly. To his horror, he saw that he had rings fixed over his eyes that blocked his eyelids and also that he no longer had a skullcap.

His brain was completely exposed and some wires were sticking out of his head. Instinctively he tried to move his hands but they too seemed to have been glued together with their palms facing downwards. He noticed a quick movement to his right.

"Alan can you hear me?"

It was not so much the sight of that being with the huge white, oval head, with two large, shiny black eyes, and seeming to float around him that startled him, but the sight of a large, brightly-edged blade clutching one of his upper limbs. He instinctively tried to scream, and from his lips the blood began to flow even more copiously. At that precise moment a small mechanical arm appeared in his field of vision and applied a new metal object to his mouth. He stared at it terrified through the mirror. The strange creature to his left lifted his chin, clenching his jaws, and as soon as his teeth clicked together, in a fraction of a second, new metal staples inserted themselves between his gums and teeth, this time much larger, to lock both arches. Now only the tears that flowed from his eyes could testify to all his excruciating suffering.

Another quick movement, this time to the left.

"Alan wake up."

He saw the blade sparkle as it fell.

It stuck a few centimetres above his pubis, then moved upwards and that expressionless being made an incision of about twenty centimetres. He never imagined he could feel such pain until that being thrust one of its limbs directly into his belly.

"You are free Alan."

Suddenly he realised he could move his arms again and instinctively brought them up to navel level but could not grab hold of anything.

"Alan you are free. Wake up now."

And as a pain-stricken Alan lost consciousness, at the same instant the same Alan woke up, still lying on a stretcher. This time, however, there were no strange creatures at his side but four smiling men who were congratulating each other. He looked at them in curiosity.

There was one dressed as a doctor laughing and high-fiving a guy with a belly and two others hugging each other.

"Where the hell am I, is this the asylum?" - he asked.

A half-truth

It was past five in the afternoon. This time it had been even longer and more complicated than the other times as Benji had encountered enormous difficulties in waking the boy up. Initially, everything had gone smoothly, but in the end Alan was in real danger of dying, one step away from a cardiac arrest that now seemed inevitable. This time it was Sergeant Carter who had the right intuition. Initially, Alan seemed to have calmed down and carried on with his story without showing any obvious emotion. But then he began to violently wriggle back onto the stretcher. Benji had tried everything to calm him down, but he continued to talk, wriggling relentlessly. David, who up to that point had been standing on the couch while Dylan and Anthony tried to keep the boy from falling to the floor, had the right idea. He hypothesised that it would be better to free Adam from that strange robe that restricted his movement. Benji quickly grasped what he was thinking, namely that it was precisely that state of constraint in real life that was reinforcing his conviction that reality was what he was telling. It was in fact enough to free his arms to finally break through to his mind.

"Well done David, good shot." - Anthony thanked him, who had really had it rough this time.

Dylan gave him the usual pat on the back.

"I told the nurse we'd take care of it this time, didn't I?" - He turned smilingly towards Dr Green.

Benji was exhausted, that afternoon had literally drained him of any remaining energy. Replacing everything in his briefcase, he stretched out on the couch. Alan didn't seem to have any particular problems, in fact he was behaving exactly like anyone who suddenly wakes up from a nightmare in the middle of the night.

The only difference was that he felt particularly tired. Dylan decided that he would listen to him the next day as there would be a press conference with Martin Cooper shortly and then he would gladly go home that evening. It had been two days since he had taken a moment for himself and his family - 'One last effort guys, press conference and then all out. When we're old we'll certainly have something to tell by the fireside."

Dylan opened the door but on immediately pushed back inside.

"Now explain to me what the heck is going on." - Chief Inspector Martin Cooper burst in furiously - "We'll deal with you later at the station." - He added, pointing his index finger at Constable Thomas who had struggled not a little to keep him out of the room.

"Agent Thomas did an excellent job." - Deferred Dylan in turn and as he closed the door winked at him - "Thanks Mark, give us another 10 minutes and keep everyone out. Ah, warn Alan Baker's relatives that the boy's OK and they'll be able to see him shortly."

The first minute served to blanch the Chief Inspector's anger. Martin Cooper, despite his reputation as a gruff man with an iron temper, was in reality a very reasonable and highly intelligent person. Just past fifty, dark complexion, six feet tall and with a slight hint of a potbelly, Cooper had always known how to choose his collaborators and make the best decisions in any situation. This time, however, he was in enormous difficulty. Even from Westminster HQ they were demanding answers. That case had now become all too famous and the news, which had been relegated from the national news to the middle of the news, had now jumped straight to the front page. There was no longer any chance of holding back the press, which now had on its hands the stories of no less than three seemingly normal boys who had literally gone off the deep end. Not to mention that the police had not issued an official statement for at least ten days.

"This is Alan Baker." - He pointed in the direction of the boy who now sat quietly on the stretcher with his legs dangling - "As you can see he's more than fine."

From a large bag hanging from the stretcher, Alan had retrieved his belongings, his shoes, a windbreaker, his wallet and his smartphone with which he was fiddling.

"I don't know why he still has his mobile phone." - David hastened to say, having guessed what Dylan was thinking - "And I'm pretty sure we won't get any meaningful data from the analysis of Lisa and Sally's smartphones, should we ever find them. I haven't had any good news from the station."

"Thanks David, now let's think about what to tell the reporters out there." - Cut Dylan short - "And you, Alan. Don't try to write anything on that phone or I'll cut your hands off." - he electrocuted him instantly.

They stayed in that room for at least another half an hour as they decided to fill Chief Inspector Cooper in on everything that had happened in the last forty-eight hours, without keeping anything from him. They stood in a corner and confabulated amongst themselves, keeping their voices low so as not to be overheard by the boy. Not that Alan showed much interest in what they were telling each other as he did not take his eyes off his smartphone. Every now and then he would look at them fearfully and raise his hand to confirm that he was doing nothing wrong. They introduced both Dr Green and Professor Hunt to Martin Cooper, pointing out how the latter had played a key role in the whole affair. They then focused on the statements to be made at the press conference and decided to introduce Benji as an external consultant who was an expert on medicines, toxic substances and nootropic drugs. They decided that the news should come out of that press conference that the cause of everything was the circulation of a dangerous new narcotic. Dylan walked towards the centre of the room where Alan was standing.

'While we detain the reporters, you go to Sally and Lisa, talk to their parents and Alan's parents. You warn them that for a few days they will have to hold us up. The kids have unintentionally taken drugs," - He said, turning loudly to David - "And in any case avoid talking to the press and anyone else outside of here."

"The same goes for you." - He added in a firm tone, pointing his finger at Alan.

"Also, you will now walk out that door lying on your gurney and, when you pass among the reporters down the hall on your way to your room, you will not make any statements but merely wave and smile." - and added - "Do we understand each other?"

Alan nodded without uttering a word.

Dylan smiled at him - "Don't worry, kid, I'll see you tomorrow."

When Alan left the room he still didn't know whether to be more relieved or more worried.

No breaks, Inspector Walker!

The press conference went smoothly. The funniest part was to see how stunned the journalists were when a triumphant and smiling Alan walked among them without showing any problems. None of them had entertained the possibility that the three boys were all right and so most of their questions were dismissed before the start. Martin Cooper posted two officers to guard the entrance to the corridor where the three boys now stood and set up four-hour shifts so that no one who was not authorised could pass. David had completed his last task of yet another long day and, on leaving the hospital, decided it was time to visit his mother for dinner. Dylan had told him that his presence during the meeting with the reporters would not be necessary.

"Not bad." - he thought. It was just after seven in the evening when the press conference, set up in record time in a room adjacent to F389, ended. The journalists were all busy, some writing the piece for the evening edition of the news or for the next day's newspaper, others on the phone communicating directly with the newsroom. Chief Inspector Martin Cooper had finally calmed down even though he was well aware that under that pile of extinguished ashes there were still some embers burning all too brightly. The girl with whom Dr Green had been having an affair for about a year, and who had now given him up for lost, had also turned up at the hospital. The two decided to spend a quiet evening in one of Hackbridge's finest restaurants and extended the invitation to Dylan and Benji. Professor Hunt gladly accepted as, although he was particularly tired, he had no desire to go cooped up in four walls inside his hotel room again. Dylan declined the invitation, glad to finally be able to go home for dinner, where the three little Walkers were certainly waiting for him with open arms.

"Daddy we saw you on TV!" - Janet, John and Jack greeted him in chorus as soon as he set foot on the doorstep.

He was showered with kisses and hugs. As soon as he managed to extricate himself, he took off his coat, placed the leather briefcase on the chest under the coat rack and headed straight for the kitchen where, waiting for him, was not only Sara but also that sly Jack Sparrow. He could have bet anything that he would still find him in the house - "Wait for the dust to settle and then I'll take over again." - he said with a smile turned to Sara as he pointed to the dog with the index finger of his right hand. A glance at the clock was enough for him to understand his children's enthusiasm as it was about twenty thirty and the news must have already made the front page on the news.

"You made a great impression dear." - Sara read his mind - "Congratulations."

Dylan merely smiled but added nothing more. At that moment he only felt like putting the whole day behind him. He could finally savour the sweet family atmosphere and the good food his wife cooked. At dinner Dylan wanted to hear from the little ones about everything they had missed over the last few days, while Sarà surprised him at the end of the meal by bringing to the table the classic tiramisu, an Italian dessert of which she was very proud and of which David also had a sweet tooth.

"Grandma Marta's recipe never betrays!" - said Sara visibly happy.

"I don't know if David will be more upset tomorrow for not being on TV or for missing this marvel." - Dylan added with a giggle - "I think I'll tell him about it."

Twenty-two-thirty came, a little later than usual, when the three little brats said goodbye to their father and went to bed. Sara had just finished tidying up the kitchen and joined Dylan in the living room where he briefly mentioned what had happened but without going into details. In reality his aim was to tell her about the people he had met over the last few days and with whom he was getting on very well. Dylan was a loner, he liked to spend his free time with his family or he enjoyed reading. To have met people with whom, on the skin of his teeth, he felt in harmony was a great novelty for him. Only David had managed to win him over, he spent wonderful days with him, but he was a long-standing friend and he now felt that he was part of his family. He told her about Professor Hunt and how he had also formed a very good relationship with Dr. Green.

"Well, it's always good to know a good doctor".

It was just as Sara spoke those words that the house phone rang. This was not a good sign. They had agreed, despite the fact that they exclusively used smartphones to communicate, to continue to have a landline at home, which, especially at night, could be useful in case of an emergency. It was certainly not a pleasure to occasionally receive calls during the day from advertising agencies or market research institutes, but that was a problem that had only manifested itself over the past year, as their number had ended up in one of those online telephone directory sites. However, those few times the phone had rung during night hours had never brought good news.

"I'll get it." - Dylan said, heading for the cordless phone resting on the shelf fixed above the television set.

"Hello?"

"Congratulations, Inspector Walker." - replied a deep, male voice from the other end of the line - "I didn't think you were perceptive enough to solve the case in such a short time."

"Look, I don't know who you are but everything we had to say we said in the press conference." - Dylan put off dryly.

"Not everything." - he resumed in a very calm voice.

After a pause for effect - 'Are you that hypnosis expert or that... Professor Hunt? Yes, I think that's the name of that guy from the United States. Don't keep me in suspense, whose credit is it?

He paused further with Dylan who found himself suddenly unable to articulate any response.

'Eh yeah... really good. I don't deny that I'm particularly angry with you for messing up all my plans. But we can see about creating a new story together with a new ending. Don't you think so?"

"Who are you? And what do you want from me?" - were the only questions that popped into Dylan's mind.

"Nothing, for now I just wanted to congratulate you. You'll have new news soon. Have a good evening, Inspector." - With those words the call was interrupted.

Dylan sat down on the couch, the cordless phone still in his hand, and tried to think as fast as he could. He already knew that he was going to spend that night alone as well, but he thought it best not to mention it to anyone until the next day. At least David and Martin Cooper would have plenty of time to rest. Sara had not yet said anything and merely looked at him. She looked at him again and noticed that his face showed all her concern. He decided, despite himself, that it was time to update her on what he had told her so far. While she was telling Sara what had happened, she sent a message to David asking him to come to the office at 8 a.m. recommending that he be punctual and then to Dr. Green announcing that she would contact him mid-morning. He made eye contact with Sara and they decided that perhaps it was time to go to bed. Dylan had no more doubts, it was going to be another long night. The next morning, at eight o'clock on the dot, not a second earlier, David arrived at the station.

"Good morning, Archie."

"Good morning, David. No vending machine today and straight to the boss's office."

"Not a good morning then..." - he said softly as he made his way to his desk.

Time to take off his jacket, put down his purse and he walked briskly towards the door at the end of the corridor. Through the inner window he could see Dylan standing inside while Chief Inspector Cooper sat at his desk with copies of the major newspapers in front of him. He knocked and without waiting for a reply entered - "Good morning everyone.". This was not a good situation at all. Dylan had waited for his arrival to bring them both up to speed on the phone call he had received the previous evening.

"Inspector Walker." - Martin Cooper paused briefly - "You know very well that we have never had the chance to get to know each other in depth but I think you really do have a sixth sense for these particular situations. Many have praised you to me. I must also note that, in spite of everything, the result we have achieved is thanks to you and, from what I have been able to ascertain, was anything but a foregone conclusion.". He picked up one of the newspapers - "The press will give us a bit of a break, but we have to restrict the number of those who will be made aware of the facts to a minimum. You have certainly thought about how to act, haven't you, Inspector?" - he paused further as if to gauge Dylan's reaction to his question - "I'm giving you carte blanche. Tell me what you need and how you want to proceed."

"I thank you for your trust but, as of today, there is not much to be done. I am sincere. This madman hasn't committed any missteps and we haven't the faintest idea who he might be. In truth, we don't even know where to start." - he began to walk nervously from one side of the room to the other while David took a seat in one of the two armchairs in front of the desk - "The only thing we can do is to try to intervene more promptly. I propose to create a small team, composed of trusted elements, and active around the clock.".

"How many men do you need, Inspector? And above all, whom do you trust blindly? I remind you that nothing is to be leaked outside of here."

"For the moment I only need twelve men to create three teams of four officers who, in eight-hour shifts, will cover the entire day. Among them I definitely want Agents Thomas and Harris."

"I would also add Archie Patel, Dylan. It's not like he's that experienced in field work, but he's certainly more than trustworthy." - David intervened.

"Well, I'll leave it to David to choose the other components since he knows most of the agents better than I do. To see if we can trust them there is only one way. Put them to the test. But we don't have time for testing, boss." - Dylan concluded.

"Agreed, Inspector."

"I also need a written request for Professor Hunt. We can't let him leave just yet. I'd say we can start with a week, transportation, room and board expenses paid by the department."

"Anything else?" - sighed Inspector Cooper, who always twisted his mouth when it came to financial demands.

"No, nothing else." - And turning to David - "Guess where we're going?"

"To James Barry's Hospital. I dream about that place at night now." - Puffed David.

"Yeah, but this time we're reversing roles. While I have a chat with Alan you brief our friends on the latest developments."

Nothing new

At James Barry's Hospital, David found himself alone, sitting at a coffee table in building F, waiting for Anthony and Benji to arrive. Dr. Green was due to start his shift at eleven o'clock and had warned him that he would drop by the hotel first to pick up Professor Hunt. He had assured him that they would arrive a few minutes early but David had other thoughts as he watched the young barmaid approach the table with a double lemon pancake, sprinkled with icing sugar. At the same moment that David was nibbling on his pancake Dylan made his entrance into corridor number seven on the third floor of the same building. He was happy to see the two officers still guarding the entrance and especially happy to find a more relaxed atmosphere. Along the corridor were the boys' parents talking to each other. He promised himself that he should compliment Anthony on the excellent organisation. He had had a room allocated for the two girls, one for young Alan and three other rooms for the six adults. That wing of the hospital had practically become a kind of hotel. The boys had been told that they would not be discharged until the following Monday at the earliest, although Alan was in excellent condition and Lisa was recovering rapidly. The decision was therefore dictated more by investigative necessity than by the health condition of the patients, and Dr Green was therefore asked to make the hospital stay as easy as possible. As soon as they became aware of the inspector's presence, everyone came to him. They had had plenty of time to exchange views on what had happened and, from the way they spoke, it seemed as if they had put almost all the pieces of the puzzle together. Dylan hastened to remind them to keep as quiet as possible about the events that had taken place and not to speak to anyone else outside that corridor - "There may be other boys in trouble and it will also depend on your behaviour how well the investigation goes." - he spoke in a calm but firm tone - "We already have a lot to think about. So let's avoid unnecessary false alarms and overly curious journalists. Clear?"

"Very clear Inspector Walker. After what you have done, you can ask us anything." - Agatha Smith intervened.

"Good. Now I would prefer to be alone with Alan." - And as she spoke she reached the boy's room.

He entered and closed the door behind him. The chat with Alan Baker did not bear the hoped-for fruit as the boy led a normal life, had a good job and enjoyed, from time to time, some recreation with friends. Alan was perfectly fit, sitting in a chair with a laptop resting on the coffee table and surfing the Internet using the hospital's WiFi connection. Surely that was one of the privileges that had been granted by Dr Green.

"Hi Alan, this is Inspector Dylan Walker." - He hastened to introduce himself with a smile.

He had immediately realised that the boy was uncomfortable from the moment he saw him - "Shall we have a quiet chat?"

They talked for about an hour. Alan had almost no recollection of what had happened to him and was amazed when Dylan asked him about his Watford and especially when he asked him if he had ever intended to follow his team to the away match at Stamford Bridge against Chelsea. Alan pulled his wallet out of his pocket and pulled out a blank piece of paper with a purchase receipt printed on it. He handed it to Dylan who could clearly read the purchase confirmation, Chelsea - Watford, Stamford Bridge, 4/5 May 2019.

A booking for three seats.

"Being a weekend game the date is not yet final but it should be played on 4 or 5 May. I bought the tickets online three days ago and printed it out just to show my friends."

"Tim and Andrew?"

Alan was increasingly amazed at how much that inspector already knew - "Yes, they're coming to watch the game too."

"Are you going on the day itself or are you planning to get to London the day before?"

"Honestly, we haven't considered arriving the day before as the ticket is already very expensive, Tim doesn't currently work and then London is not that far from Watford. The journey will take just over an hour." - Reflected Alan - "No, I'd say we'll do it all in a day."

"Alright Alan." - Dylan made to get up - "Now one last thing. Follow me."

Dylan walked out of the room and continued down the corridor, asking the others present to keep their distance. Alan followed him like a shadow. When he reached the two girls' door he knocked on the jamb and waited for their invitation to enter.

"Hello girls, how are you?"

Sally was obviously still a little sore but had recovered very well in that short time, while Lisa was all in good shape.

"Inspector Walker, I've brought you company. This is Alan." - he said, putting a hand on the boy's left shoulder and pushing him forward a little - "Don't they eat you?" - she smiled.

The two girls smiled back as Alan's cheeks coloured. Dylan had a definite goal and felt he needed to create a cheerful atmosphere - "Now let's play a game, you'll be here for another week anyway and you have to find a way to pass the time." - He turned towards Alan - "Then there are two pretty girls and I'd say smartphones and computers can wait for a while, right?"

"Yes, of course inspector." - he hastened to reply, lowering his gaze and looking more shy than he had initially appeared to be.

"From now on you will start talking to each other, talking about yourselves and above all remembering everything you have done in the last month. I want you to carefully examine your lives until you find any point of contact. This is important for the investigation and I want you to put all the effort you can into it."

He turned to the girls - "We already know that you two were at the London Roman Museum the first weekend in February. Right?"

Lisa and Sally nodded. Dylan then turned directly to Sally - "Sally I know you're not in perfect condition yet but I also know you can do it. Take it as a game, a pastime. But do it."

She waited for any objections and, before taking her leave, added - "I'll come by as soon as I can to see if you have any news. If, on the other hand, you think you've found a really interesting coincidence... well, in that case let me contact you right away."

As soon as he stepped out into the corridor he warned the adults present of what he had just requested of the boys, then walked off at a good pace, heading for the bar on the first floor to see if David was still in the area. He thought back to his morning meeting with the chief inspector and suddenly felt the full weight of responsibility for the case on his shoulders. Martin Cooper had given him carte blanche for the second time in less than a week. He had made some very specific demands, but he was aware that he would need a new stroke of luck to find the crux of the matter. He had no idea what else to do and how to proceed with the investigation. He admitted to himself that he was at an impasse. Over the next few days the situation did not improve. Nothing relevant happened and the more time passed, the more he became aware that the fuse was about to end. Something was going to happen.

But when?

Unfortunately, the investigation was at a standstill, the guys from James Barry's Hospital had found no further leads to follow and Chief Inspector Cooper was back to being as grumpy as he had been during the previous fire weekend. They tried on Friday evening to defuse the tension by organising a dinner party all together, David, Anthony, his girlfriend Jenny and Benji. Of course, like every Friday night, they were all gathered at the Walker house for Sara's famous pizza and, despite the tension, Dylan was happy to introduce his new friends to his wife and his little brats. Ah, of course Jack Sparrow was there too, always busy with his search for crumbs which, coincidentally, always fell by little Janet's chair. It was a very successful evening with Benji and David turning up with their loads of beer, while Anthony and Jenny had taken care of bringing dessert. Dr Green had resumed his normal duties at James Barry's Hospital and it had been two days since he had even looked out on the third floor to check on the three boys. They were in good hands and, apart from Sally, the other two could have left the hospital long ago. In any case, they would all be discharged on Monday and Benji had already booked the ten o'clock flight that would take him back to Cambridge, in the United States, to resume his university chair. He had given his full willingness to return to England should the need arise but he did not want to miss any more lectures for a wait that no one could say for sure how many more days it was destined to last. That evening he was enraptured by Sara's pizza, which managed to present a range of variations to make any pizzeria envious.

"Excellent, really excellent." - he repeated each time he tasted a new piece - "Then this capricciosa pizza is absolutely divine!"

"Sara, you know how you love your cooking. If Dylan hadn't married you I would have, but..." - David turned towards Benji - "It doesn't take that much to impress someone who's used to putting pineapple on their pizza, does it?"

A good friendship had developed between David and Benji. They had two similar characters and were able, depending on the moment, to be both very professional and like kids ready to bicker about anything. Both of them were also always able to find the right words to break up stressful or highly embarrassing situations.

"Separated at birth. No more doubts." - said Dylan laughing.

That evening was realistically the high point of the week. Not least because the next day, Saturday 2 March 2019, the situation was set to go downhill. Dylan had not gone to the office as he still had to recover from the previous weekend spent in hospital. The day passed very peacefully until, shortly after eight o'clock in the evening, he received another phone call at home. It was Sara who answered and Dylan understood everything as soon as he saw his wife's face turn immediately serious.

"Give my best wishes to your husband, Mrs Walker. That's all he said to me, Dylan, then he ended the call." - Sara reported.

At the same moment the smartphone also rang and David's name began to flash on the screen.

"Dylan we need to rush to the hospital, we have a new case. There are already four officers on the scene." - she warned him - "In the meantime I'll contact both Benji and Anthony. I'm already on my way. Get ready for me to pick you up."

"Very good, David." - he said.

"Very bad, Dylan." - He thought as he walked towards the room.

Vicky Williams

"So what news do we have?" - Dylan promptly asked as he got into the car.

"Bad, very bad, Dylan." - began David as he picked up speed in the direction of James Barry's Hospital - "Vicky Williams, 38 year old resident of Woodley in the county of Berkshire. From what Constable Harris told me, she was narrowly saved. They had just arrived when they saw her drop dead weight into the River Wandle. He and his partner had to work hard to get her safely back to the levee."

He paused, biting his lower lip.

"What else is there David?" - Dylan sensed that the worst part of the tale was yet to come.

"The alarm was raised by two reporters from a local paper. From what John told me, the two were alerted in the late afternoon by an anonymous phone call. A male voice urged them to report at 7.45pm on Culvers Avenue, at the height of the bridge over the River Wandle. He added that they would find a girl acting strangely".

David went on to explain how the two journalists, each unaware of the other's presence, had met on the bridge. They had both thought of a mythomaniac and therefore had not seen fit to alert the police in advance. Moreover, the cases of the three boys, who had animated the previous weekend, had been dismissed and neither had thought there might be a connection, at least until that moment.

"As soon as they arrived they noticed, over the parapet of the bridge, a girl standing motionless and poised on the embankment. Only then did they decide to call the emergency services. Fortunately, Constable Harris was on patrol in the area and was therefore able to intervene in time to save her,' he explained. - David explained in one breath - "I think we'll be on the front page tomorrow with a nice photo shoot as well."

In front of the entrance to James Barry's Hospital were already a dozen journalists, well armed with cameras and microphones.

"We have nothing to declare." - were Dylan's only words as he proceeded with difficulty towards the entrance.

"Are you still confirming our version of the new narcotic, or did you hide something?"

"How is it possible that someone knew in advance what was going to happen?"

"You know very well that you will have to explain the anonymous phone call to us.".

"Answer, Inspector!"

A couple of officers, the second from the night shift, intervened to help him through the entrance and then blocked everyone else outside the large entrance window. After a couple of minutes he was joined by David who, after parking, had to undergo the same treatment in order to enter the hospital.

He saw Dylan who had just interrupted a phone call - "Damn, that's all we need is Cooper! Let's go David." - and set off in the direction of the emergency room via the inner corridors.

Anthony was already there waiting for them - "My shift would be over by nine o'clock." - and opened the door inviting them in - "Come on, I just got here too. I've been busy in the operating theatre."

Inside the emergency room the situation was very quiet. Vicky Williams was lying on a stretcher, motionless, an IV connected to her left arm and a nurse feeling her pulse. One of the two doctors on duty approached them.

"No vital parameters thrown off, everything negative. When she arrived here at the hospital the nurses said she was very calm even in the ambulance." - then after a pause he added - "You know the story of Sleeping Beauty? You could say she's in a coma but I don't think she is. She has no response to verbal stimuli and no reaction even to painful stimuli. I don't know if I explained myself..." - he said as with a complicit look he turned to Dr Green.

"Clear and concise. This is Dr Thompson, a person who enjoys my utmost confidence and one of the few who knows what really happened on the third floor." - Anthony hastened to explain - "I'd say we're good to go, Benji should be here in a bit, too."

"On that desk we put his personal belongings. Agent Harris also took care of retrieving everything the girl had in her wallet, as it was all wet. He also told me to let you know that he would be waiting for you directly on the third floor." - Before saying goodbye he added - "Ah, as usual we have arranged for the family to be notified."

"Thank you Dr Thompson. David take care of it, we'll be on our way in the meantime." - He turned on his heel, opened the door and walked out at a good pace followed by Anthony as Dr Thompson instructed a nurse to transfer the patient.

"Wait for me before you start!" - David hastened to say as he approached the desk.

"Can I take it?" - he asked, turning to a nurse sitting nearby and intent on filling out forms.

"Sure, we have lots of them." - she replied, pointing to a stack that contained at least fifteen other large blue plastic trays.

David began to gently carry all the objects and papers scattered on the table onto that tray.

He started from his right, trying to place everything roughly in the same way as it had been arranged on the desk. First the wallet, then the banknotes, some old receipts, the identity card, a couple of business cards, a hardware store and a restaurant, and a few sheets of paper with notes that were now illegible. Then he moved on to the smartphone, an old Samsung model that would probably never be switched on again, its hard plastic case, a ticket for a show and a soggy packet of tissues.

He walked out waving goodbye and headed for the lift - "Come on Dylan, wait for me, I'm coming... I can't miss it." - he thought as he cast one more eye over the pile of soggy objects that threatened to blow his session. Then something caught his attention.

"This is not new to me..." - he said to himself as he took the ticket back in his hands - "Irish Circus of Mystery, Friday 1 March 2019, first performance twenty o'clock, industrial estate, Reading."

A bell-like sound alerted him to the fact that he had reached the floor, he stepped out and headed for Aisle 8.

"Damn!" - he exclaimed when he saw the door to room F389 already closed, with Agent Harris and one of his colleagues already manning it - "You're paying for this one Dylan."

He sat down in the first chair he came across and huffing returned to look at the note.

Acrophobia

She couldn't quite remember how she got into that mess. And even if she wanted to, how could she?

The first time she had seen them she had been breathless. They had described to her in detail those bright green, almost fluorescent meadows she would have encountered as she drove along the typical Irish lanes leading to the Cliffs of Moher, the imposing cliffs near the village of Doolin, which reached heights of more than 200 metres, overhanging the sea. But nothing could have prepared her for the sight of such a spectacle. It had been a long journey but well worth it. Even before she reached the cliffs, Vicky Williams could already hear the roar of the waves crashing violently against the rock from below, creating white clouds that were blown skyward by the bold wind blowing across the ocean ridges. The air was cold and full of that typical taste of the sea. That was all she could remember, and even trying hard she could not explain how she could find herself standing there on a rocky outcrop no more than six inches wide, overlooking the sea and precariously balanced. Below her, a drop of over a hundred and fifty metres separated her from the water.

Diiinnnn!

And then there was that sound that was pounding in her temples, as full as the tolling of a bell but with such frequency that it was driving her mad. Her back was pressed against the rock. She could comfortably move her head only by looking downwards, but she soon realised that all it took was a small shift in her centre of gravity to feel her shoulders immediately pull away from the wall. Above her, safety was no more than five metres away but her calls for help were overpowered by the din coming from below. She had now realised that she had no hope of getting out of the situation alive. She was stuck in a spot above a small inlet and below her, at the point where the rough waters cleared, sharp-pointed rocks rose up.

"I'll end up right on those rocks." - she repeated to herself over and over again.

She had long since stopped trying to call for help. Her throat was burning and the air that smelled salty did nothing to improve matters. The tears that sprang from her eyes pooled below her chin and, after a short dance, they joined together and launched themselves into the void, finally free, to reach the ocean. Vicky could not even remember how long she had been there, hovering, one step away from death. By now she felt tired, too tired.

Diiinnnn!

"Oh, no! Stop please!" - she kept hearing that damn sound in her ears.

It was unbearable, her head was exploding. She couldn't take it any longer. She closed her eyes. She prayed intensely and thought of her father who had so lovingly raised her.

"Mama, I'm coming." - And she leaned forward, launching herself into the void.

"Wake up Vicky." - Benji said sharply as he tapped some sort of tuning fork one last time on what looked like a small steel rod.

Vicky Williams jolted awake. This time she had not used the usual pendulum. She had explained to Dylan and Anthony that she would resort to a new technique given the girl's state.

"Don't worry Vicky, everything is fine." - Dr Green quickly reached her - "You're at James Barry's Hospital in Hackbridge."

"What happened? I don't remember anything." - Vicky looked around suspiciously.

"Don't worry, it's OK now." - Benji reassured her.

"Congratulations Professor Hunt." - Dylan intervened, throwing a smile in Vicky's direction - "Less than 40 minutes and this gorgeous girl is already in tip-top shape."

"Yeah, but it wasn't like the other times." - he hastened to point out.

Benji cast a quick glance at Anthony, who understood on the fly.

"Now come on, Vicky. You need to rest. Your loved ones should be arriving shortly." - He took the stretcher, opened the door and led Vicky out of the room.

He was stopped on the threshold by David, who leaned over the girl, murmuring something to her.

He waited for the girl's reply and then took the opportunity to look out - "Are you done yet?"

He got no answer. He gave Agent Thomas a quick glance to make sure he was still standing guard at the door, went inside and closed it. Benji was as usual intent on tidying up his tools of the trade.

"My opinion is that this time there was not a great deal of care taken by the hypnotist in creating her virtual environment. The girl had less detailed vision and her memories were short and presented too many gaps."

"Maybe she didn't have time to do a precise job like with the other kids." - Dylan tried to speculate.

"Maybe but I think otherwise." - She fixed him with a serious look - "I could bet on it. This time the ending had to be a girl drowned in the River Wandle."

Dylan gritted his teeth. Indeed that was a possibility to be seriously considered.

'Actually... it was just a fluke that there was a patrol nearby.' - he thought aloud.

They really were in deep trouble.

"Besides, this time I got confirmation of what I already suspected." - Benji sat back in his chair and leaned against the backrest with his hands clasped behind his neck.

"I am referring to the notice given to the two reporters. We are dealing with someone capable of producing effects even after a long time on the mind of their victim." - he took a further reflective pause - "And also with frightening precision. Undoubtedly an insane but extremely capable person. I honestly didn't think one could cross certain boundaries."

Dylan pounded a fist on the desk, then leaned back with both hands, arms outstretched and head bowed, pondering his next moves.

"Dylan." - David interrupted him. His friend replied only with a weak nod.

"I know this may be stupid and have nothing to do with the case but among Vicky's belongings I found this." - And he placed the circus ticket on the desk, right before Dylan's eyes.

"Yes David, we're all going to work at the circus in a bit.".

A few seconds of absolute silence passed. Strange.

David's reply was slow in coming. He was certainly not the type to pass up the opportunity to engage in a pointless conversation with the aim of bringing some serenity to a tense situation. Dylan raised his head and slowly shifted his gaze in her direction.

"I've seen that circus before, or at least seen what was left of it." - David began his tale by explaining how he had already seen those images in the billboards in the car park outside the Roman London Museum.

"It could just be a coincidence. After all, I figured no one would be naive enough to leave such a heavy clue on the girl. Let alone someone as smart as our madman. But..."

"But what David?" - Dylan urged.

"Though, while I was waiting outside the door here, Inspector Harris told me he didn't find that note inside Vicky's wallet but it was stored in a narrow slot, behind the smartphone... that is, wedged between the smartphone and the hard case."

"Continue David.".

"I don't know... Outside I had time to think. Maybe I thought that the fact that smartphones sometimes disappear and instead other times we find them is because... maybe... in some cases they could have revealed some clue to us, maybe a photo or a video..." - he didn't notice that he had started walking nervously around the room, just as Dylan was used to doing - "Oh, and then I asked Vicky about it, here in the doorway. It looked good to me and I took the opportunity to ask her about why she kept that note hidden on the back of the phone."

"Continue." - Dylan had now come within half a metre of David.

"She reported to me that whenever she goes into a place where there's an entrance ticket, she used to keep it back there, for fear of losing it and that someone might ask for it after she got in."

"David, call the station and have them confirm the exact date the circus was in front of the Roman London Museum and tell you where it is now." - Dylan headed for the exit and motioned the two to follow him - "Let's go find the last piece of the puzzle."

He didn't even see who was on the other side of that door and walked briskly towards corridor number 7 with David in tow, who was already on the phone, and Benji with his trusty briefcase. It was not yet nine o'clock and the three boys were all together in

Alan's room watching television. Dylan entered without announcing himself - "Irish Circus of Mystery." - He waited for the boys to turn around and repeated - "Irish Circus of Mystery. Do you know anything about it?".

Alan was the first to reply "Yes, I was there last weekend. Saturday if I remember correctly.".

"Where was the circus?"

"It was in Watford." - he replied.

Knowing that was already a big point in his favour, Dylan turned towards the two girls.

Sally shook her head as Lisa looked thoughtful.

"Lisa, what are you thinking about?" - Dylan urged her.

'A while ago, when I visited the museum, there was a circus opposite. I don't remember the exact name. I approached it because they always fascinated me but it was closed. There was only a big carriage to the right of the entrance. I can't remember well but on the side there was a drawing...".

"Of a wizard in a pointy hat bent over a crystal ball." - Sally intervened - "Now I remember it too. It was the only attraction also open during the day. Five pounds to read your palm."

"Bingo!" - Dylan exclaimed, hurriedly leaving the room.

"From the station, they confirmed the dates. The circus is now in Guildford, about eighty minutes away."

"Right David, leave four officers here on call at the hospital and advise the other eight to meet us at the station in fifteen minutes. I want Harris and Thomas with us. Archie assign him to coordinate the others in the hospital." - He looked at his watch - "We're off to

Guildford. If all goes well we'll be there in time to enjoy the grand finale.".

Mr. Mystery

It had started to drizzle. It was about twenty-two thirty and all the occupants inside Sergeant Carter's black Jeep were intent on staring at the entrance to the Irish Circus of Mystery. There was no sign of the carriage described by the girls and the street was completely deserted.

"What do you propose Inspector Walker?" - asked Chief Inspector Cooper who, having just been made aware of the latest developments, had decided to join the team.

In the car were David and Dylan in the front while in the back seats Martin Cooper sat in the middle with Benji and Anthony on either side. They had agreed to keep manpower to a minimum and all those deemed non-essential were ordered to stay at least a mile away from the circus. Only one other car was parked behind them with four officers on board, including Mark Thomas and John Harris. The medical staff, in case of need, was reduced to the presence of Dr Green alone.

"You guys wait here. I'll approach on the pretext of asking for information at the ticket office." - Dylan replied.

Through the weathered windscreen they could clearly make out Dylan walking slowly towards the ticket office.

He had borrowed David's new umbrella - "Be sure, it's new." - he told him, but knew full well that his trusty friend was referring to something else entirely. Dylan spent about a minute conversing with an elderly gentleman inside the ticket office, then walked towards the entrance and disappeared from their sight.

"I lost him boss." - said David who, even using his binoculars, could not see over the fence.

Inside the circus, Dylan walked confidently in the direction of the bandwagon, following the directions of the old ticket-taker. As a child, he too had always been fascinated by the circus, but as he grew up, he realised how wrong it was to keep those animals locked in cages. Fortunately, things had now changed and the circus was once again an interesting option for an alternative evening out. He followed the outer perimeter of the tent, taking care to dodge the cables and anchor ropes. From inside he could hear a great uproar of applause and laughter. He looked at his watch.

The show was drawing to a close - "We don't have much time." - he thought as, after one last dodge, he saw a large dark carriage appear right in front of him, about twenty metres away.

He took out his smartphone and sent a text message to David. Then he took a deep breath and began to walk circumspectly in that direction. He could now see more clearly the image imprinted on the side, the same one Lisa and Sally had described to him. He had come within ten feet when he noticed that the door was ajar. A thin beam of orange light leaked from the side crack, colouring the four steps of the wooden staircase leading to the entrance. He climbed them slowly but, although he was paying close attention, the wooden ladder creaked several times under his weight. He leaned on the side jamb as he watched carefully in the direction of the other one, the one from which the light came. He stretched out an arm and slowly opened the door. What he saw left him interjected.

"Have a seat Inspector Walker." - said the old man without even looking up from the table where he was sitting.

In front of him stood the same person he had spoken to in the ticket office. Dylan entered, took a chair to his left, walked over to the table and sat down.

"I am Mr Mystery, the owner of the circus. I welcome you inside my humble abode." - He looked up and smiled - "It may not have all the comforts of a real home, but if you want wheels underneath, you have to give something up, right?"

"Yes you're right though there is a bit of a gloomy atmosphere. Don't you think?" - Hitting back at the sender, Dylan decided to play along.

"Of course but that's part of my job. Those who come in here know they're going to get their palms read by the great Mr Mystery not an old man lying on the sofa in front of the TV. You need maniacal attention to detail to ensure that your customers find exactly what they are looking for."

Then he resumed smiling - "You should have seen his face when he opened the door... He didn't expect to find me, did he?"

"In fact, I was surprised by it. I can't deny it."

"Normally he wouldn't have recognised me, with a fake beard and that big pointy hat." - he said, pointing to the floor with his blue hat, the same one he was pictured with outside.

He leaned back with a satisfied expression and added - "No one imagines standing in front of the great Mr Mystery while standing in line for a ticket."

Dylan interrupted him - "And as soon as someone buys a ticket to meet you on this bandwagon, the conductor, that's you, entertains him by trying to squeeze as much information out of him as possible."

"That's right Inspector, a bit like I did with you. In this I am modestly the best." - He laughed heartily - "The client enters this wonderful mansion and within the first sixty seconds is already convinced that I possess who knows what powers. I already know everything about him. At that point he is ready to believe anything I tell him.".

Then he turned serious for a moment - "Hey, but I don't do anything wrong! In the end it's just talk about matters of the heart, about what the future holds, and of course, ninety-nine times out of a hundred, my predictions are more than positive."

"And that time it's not?"

"Inspector! Something... how shall I say... not pleasant... yes, not pleasant, I have to say otherwise I would lose all my credibility. For example I could tell you that you will pass your driving test but you will have some uncertainty during the test, or I could tell you that I foresee a long happy life for you but at the same time I would advise you not to take the car for the whole week so as not to get into a bad accident. Come on, nothing that could be considered a crime, right?" - he started laughing again.

That old man couldn't have been the man they were looking for and Dylan was convincing himself that he'd blown it. Maybe he had just been too rash in making the decision to go in alone. He should have acted more cautiously and instead - "Haste is bad advice." - he thought.

"What are you thinking about Inspector?" - asked old Mr Mystery.

He couldn't back out now, he had to play his cards close to his chest. He decided to stick his neck out; after all, he had not come all that way for nothing. He tried in every way to tease the old man, told him about the mystery of the River Wandle, as the press had now dubbed them. But he had no reaction. Not a single one gave in, on the contrary he showed great interest and asked several times if he could be in any way helpful in the development of the investigation. He repeated several times, laughing, that he had no power in predicting the future, but gave his utmost willingness.

Dylan leaned back tiredly - "I don't have any proof" - he thought - "And if there was any, I burned it".

Reluctantly he got up and said goodbye to old Mr Mystery. Dylan walked out of that bandwagon with the defeated expression of someone who knew he had exhausted all his resources. He had tried everything, but perhaps he had acted recklessly. He no longer had any tricks up his sleeve and knew that the worst was yet to come. Back in the car, he endured Chief Inspector Cooper's reprimand that lasted the entire journey back to Hackbridge. He had blown it and behaved like a rookie.

"Do you realise you've erased the only lead we had?" - Martin Cooper urged him - "Now it's going to be a lot more complicated to frame anyone working in that circus... if anything, that's really where we need to look."

Even David had found very few words to defend him and had driven by remaining silent until they arrived at the station. So had Benji and Anthony, who did not say a word. Everyone had expected a very different ending.

"Inspector Walker." - said Martin Cooper as he got out of the car - "I can understand that this has been a difficult time for you. Perhaps I too have been overloading you with responsibility, but tonight you have shown that you are not fit to handle such complex cases." - he paused - "As he told me in the office? That to understand whether or not you can trust a person you have to test them. Right?"

He waited in vain for an answer. Dylan sat in the car with bowed head brooding over everything that had gone wrong. There was something that didn't convince him but his thoughts struggled to make space for themselves.

"Take a week off." - said the chief inspector in a moment of calm, perhaps realising he had gone too far - "Take your family and have a holiday away from here. It can only do you good. Then on your return we'll see what we can do. OK?"

Without adding a word, Dylan nodded.

"David, tomorrow morning at seven thirty in the office." - Martin Cooper concluded before closing the door.

David was strangely silent as he drove him home. In fact, no one could find the right words to break that heavy silence.

"David I trust you." - Dylan said as he got out of the car - "You do a good job."

Then he turned to Benji and Anthony - "Hi guys and thanks for being available. Unfortunately, that's the way it went."

O.C.D.

Martin Cooper was absolutely right. He had behaved like a rookie. All Dylan could do was think about all the mistakes he had made. It wasn't like him to behave so recklessly, he just couldn't explain what was going on in his head at that moment. He couldn't help but think back to those minutes spent in front of Mr. Mystery. He realised that the Chief Inspector had also been right to recommend a rejuvenating holiday. He needed to unplug. And so it was that on Tuesday, 5 March, the entire Walker family set off on a week-long cruise to the Norwegian fjords. Sara had realised that something had gone wrong and knew that the mysteries of the River Wandle were far from solved. Dylan, however, had not mentioned anything to her and she decided to respect his silence. Updates on the cases were always in the headlines and there seemed to have been a new discovery even the night before they left. She had heard of a young man in his twenties who was admitted in serious condition and, during the last report, she had also caught sight of David's silhouette passing near the entrance to James Barry's Hospital.

"Maybe I should call David." - he had thought several times.

But Dylan showed little interest in the latest news and she avoided any talk that might have reference to his work.

Whatever had happened, a family holiday could only do everyone good, not least because it had been at least two years since they'd had one, so much so that the twins had all but forgotten the last one. And indeed, after a couple of days, things seemed to improve markedly. Dylan had spared no expense and had taken one of the nicest rooms on the ship. In reality it was almost a mini-apartment, with a small entrance area from which one could access a large master bedroom with a private bathroom, a second bathroom and a second children's room with a single bed and a bunk bed. But the most beautiful thing was the large French window that opened onto a small balcony overlooking the ocean. The first few days were quite hectic and it was difficult to agree on what to do, as there were so many activities going on at the same time in different areas of the ship. Dylan was more active and often offered to accompany the children to their special play area or to the restaurant, which was open round the clock and offered all kinds of delicacies. On Friday morning Sara left the room at nine o'clock sharp. She had made an appointment at the hairdresser's on board. She was determined. She was going to look beautiful that evening. She had already organised everything to perfection with a candlelit dinner in a small private area overlooking the fjords, while the children would be supervised by a private entertainer who would also take them to the cinema. That evening would be all about them. She left Dylan and the boys still sleeping and returned that it was almost eleven o'clock.

"What do you think of this fantastic hairstyle?" - she asked as she closed the door behind her and in the process made the gesture of stroking her hair with her right hand.

She had no answer. A shiver ran down her spine. Why the heck was it so cold?

"Dylan? Janet? Hello?" - she asked, raising her tone of voice.

She thought maybe they had all gone out as usual to have a second breakfast at the café. So she calmly entered the room but what she saw chilled her blood. Dylan was sitting, motionless, wearing only a shirt, his head bowed and clutching something in his hands. Behind him the French window was wide open and an icy wind was blowing in.

"Where are the children? Where are they?" - Sara started to shout, running towards the boys' room and then immediately looking inside the toilets.

Dylan still didn't answer. He returned to the room and his gaze fell terrified in the direction of the large window. A flash of lightning. Now everything was clear to her.

"No! Dylan no!" - she cried desperately as she stepped out onto the balcony - "Dylan what have you done to our children?"

She turned to look at him, begged for him to answer her, and it was there that he saw her. In his hands Dylan was clutching a shiny blade. He looked up at her as large tears ran down his face.

"Forgive me." - he said.

Then he raised his arm with the blade pointing towards his own chest.

"Freeze!"

"On the ground!"

"Put it down!"

"Inside, inside!"

A sudden series of orders broke the silence inside the carriage. Within seconds all the officers poured inside the room.

"Watch out, David!" - Benji, who had been the first to notice Dylan sitting in a dark corner of the room, warned him.

He had one arm raised and was holding what looked like a kitchen knife. David and Martin Cooper managed to pin him down just in time while Officers Thomas and Harris took care of handcuffing an old man who made no resistance.

'Put a hood on him and tape his mouth shut,' - Benji promptly suggested.

Then they laid Dylan on the ground. Benji opened the briefcase and pulled out his pendulum. Anthony felt his pulse.

Right.

Left.

Right.

Left.

It only took a few swings.

"Welcome back Dylan," - said Benji.

Author's notes

Any references to existing people or real events are purely coincidental.

This is a work of pure fantasy, a product of my own creativity.

Some places really exist, but their descriptions have been adapted to fit into the story.

These include the river Wandle, the beautiful Maldives islands, the fascinating city of Cairo with its pyramids, the imposing Cliffs of Moher, some of the most beautiful parks in the district of Sutton and, finally, pretty Hackbridge, where our Inspector Walker has chosen to start a family.

The South London Police District and the S.I.P. (Special Investigation Police) unit are also figments of my imagination, as are Barry's James Hospital, the Museum of Roman London and the Irish Mystery Circus.

PHOBIAS

A STRANGE CASE FOR INSPECTOR DYLAN WALKER

Copyright ©2024 – Manuel J. Spencer

ALL RIGHTS RESERVED